THE LAND OF LINES

Victor Hussenot

chronicle books · san francisco

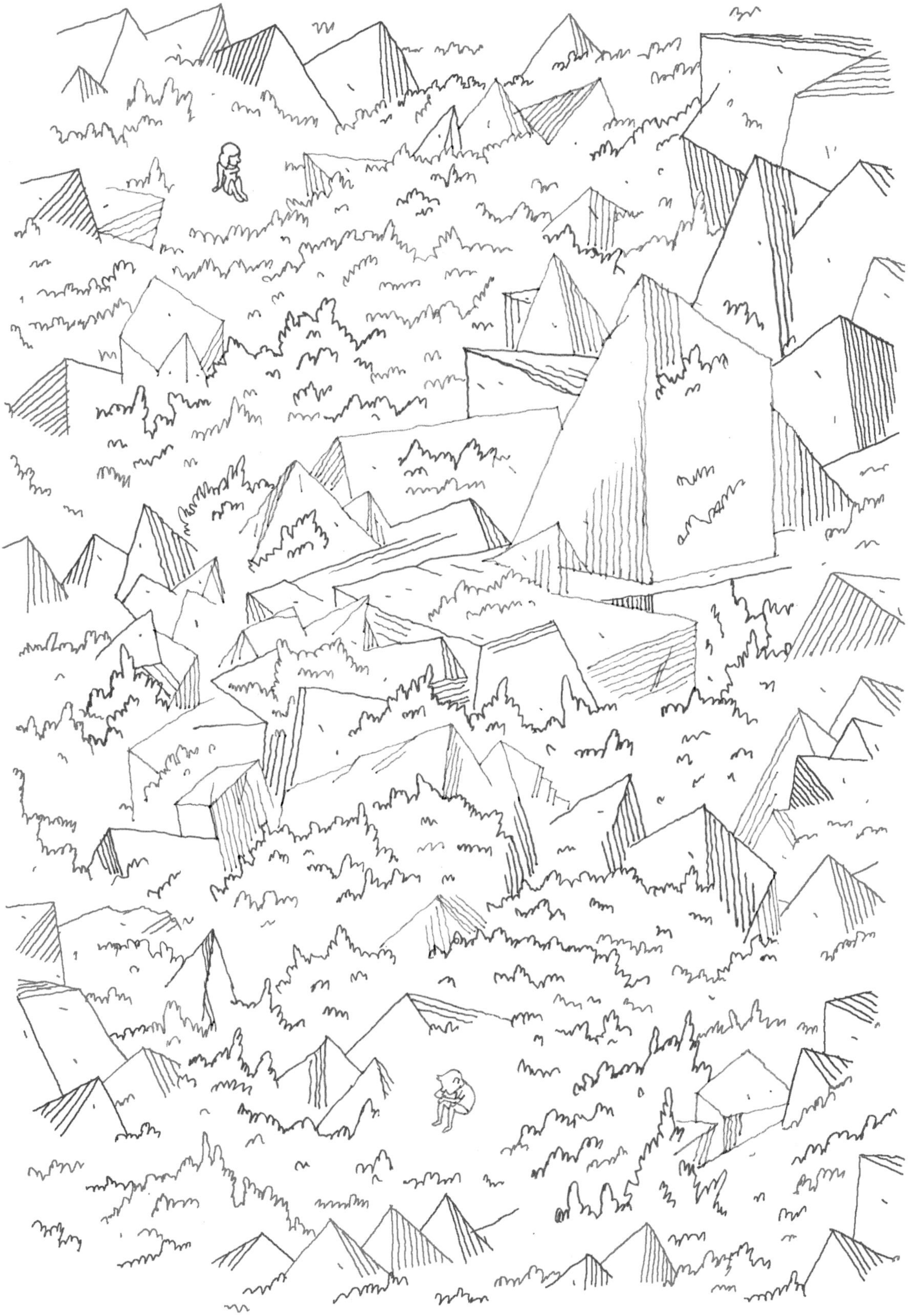

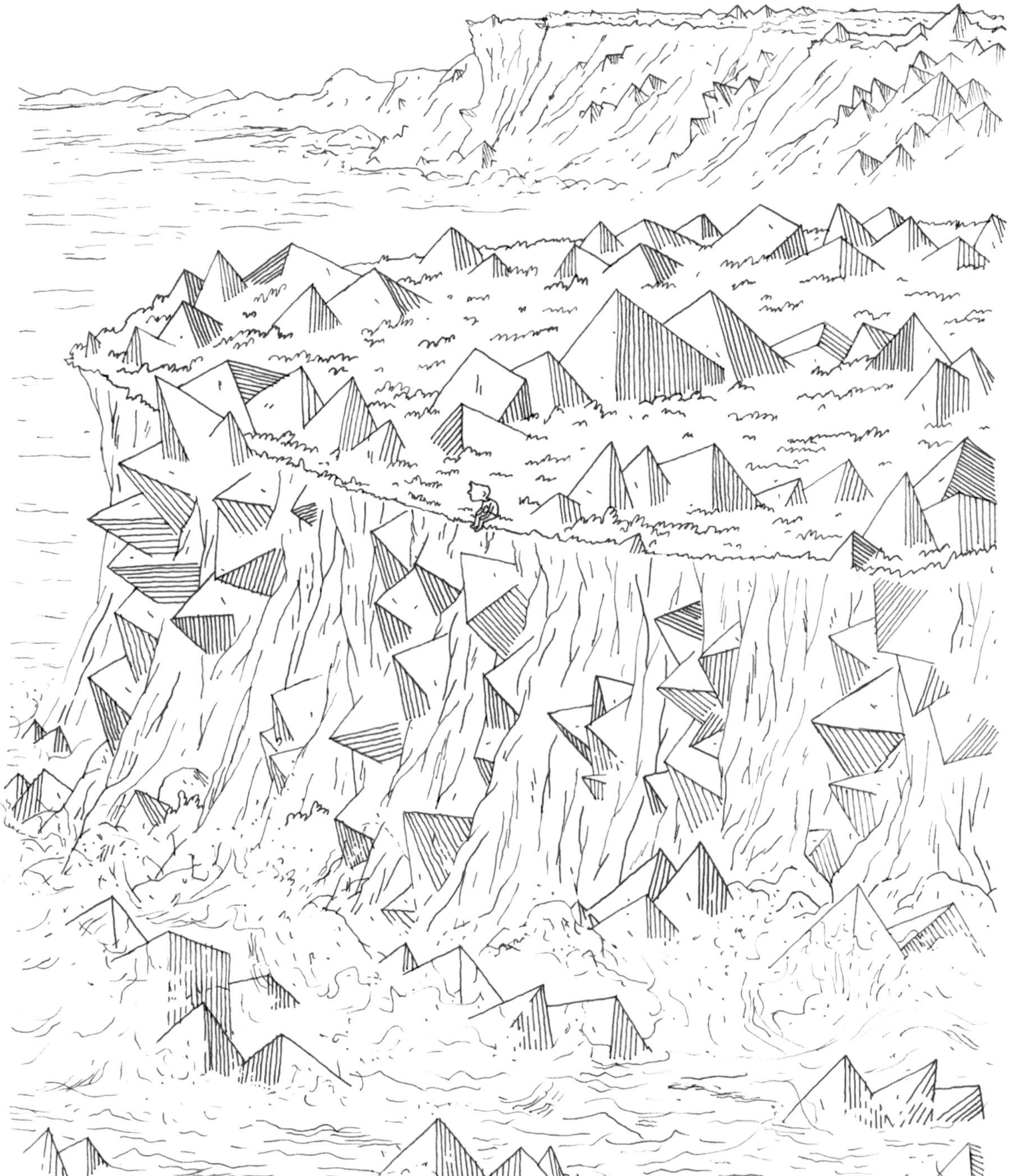

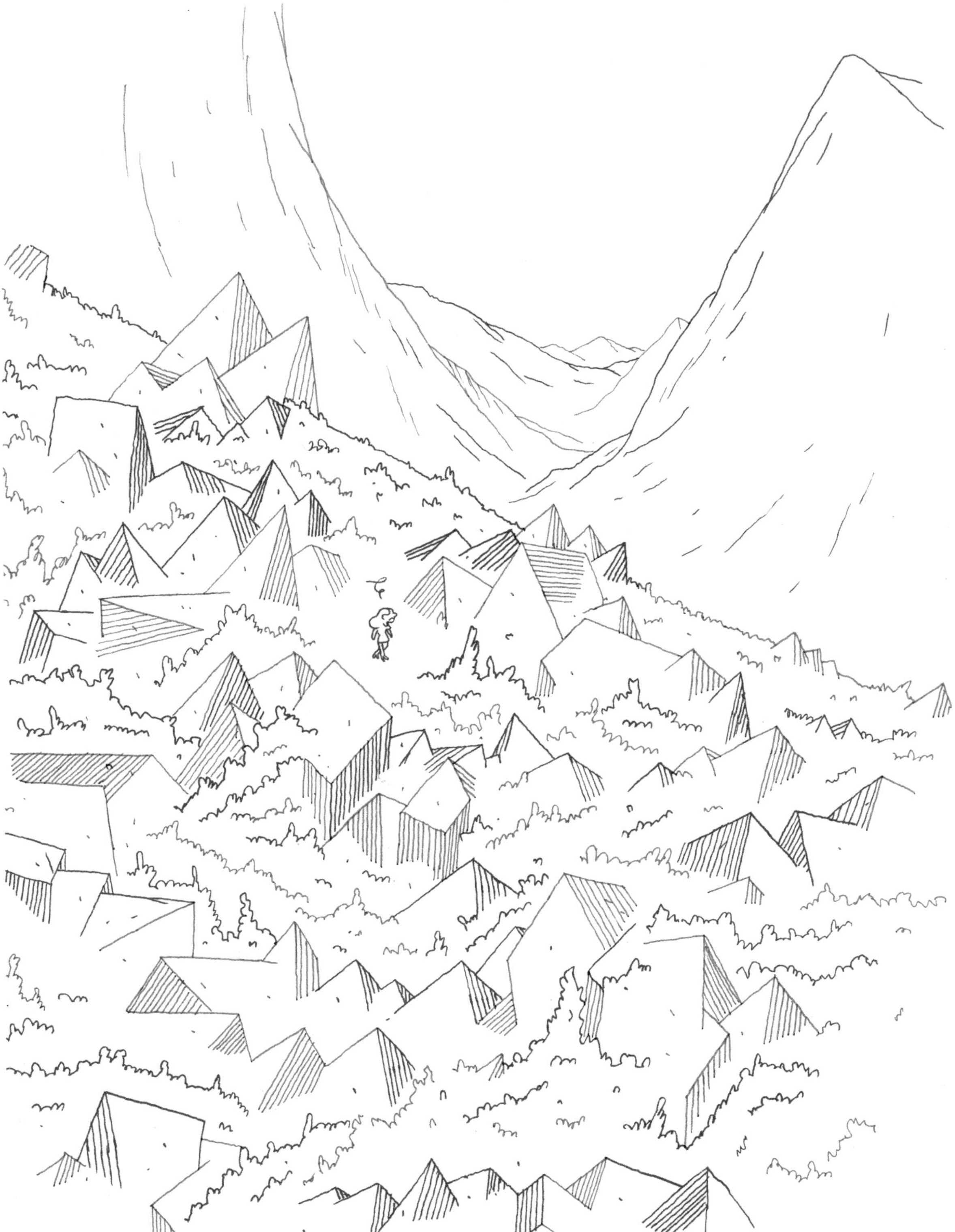

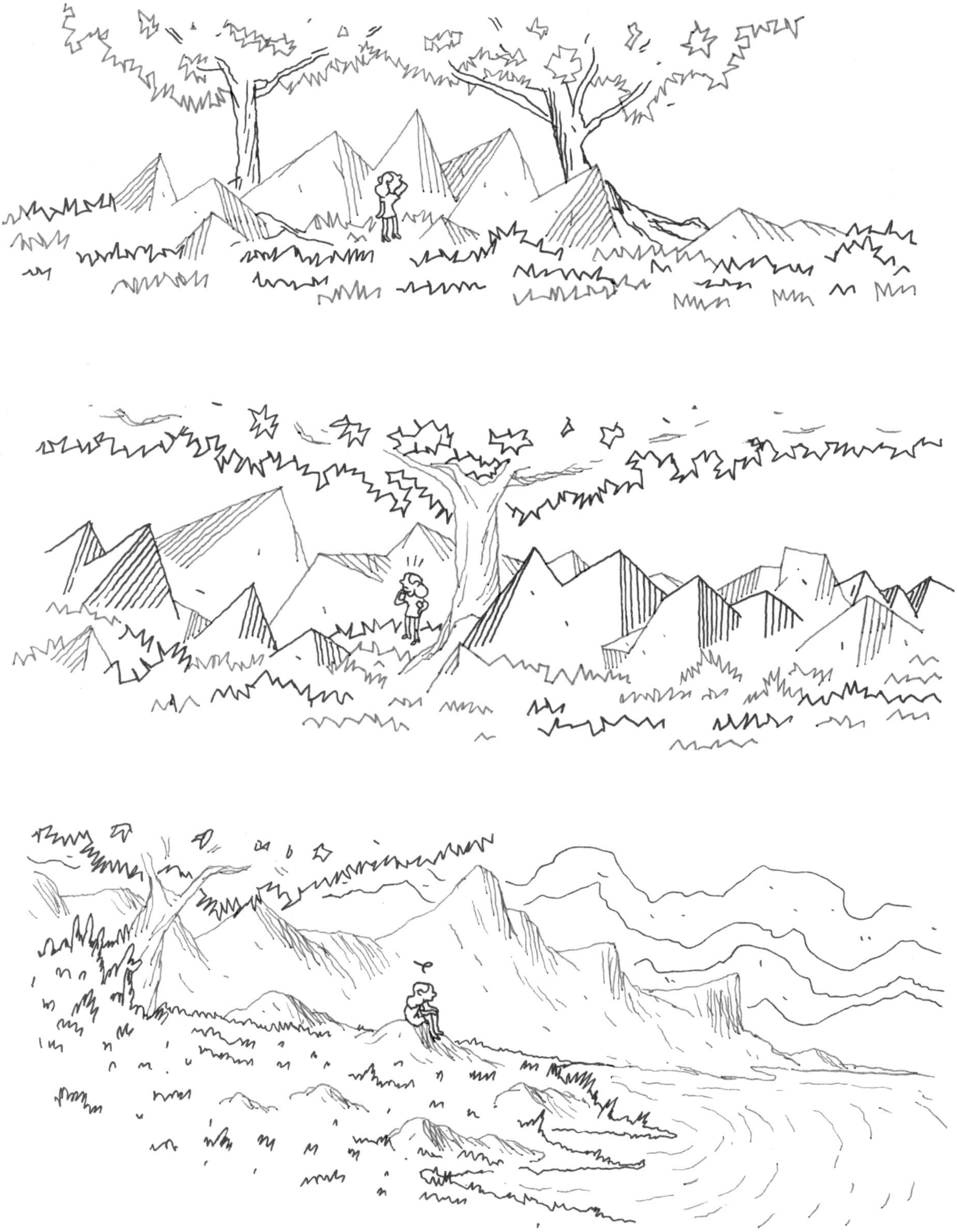

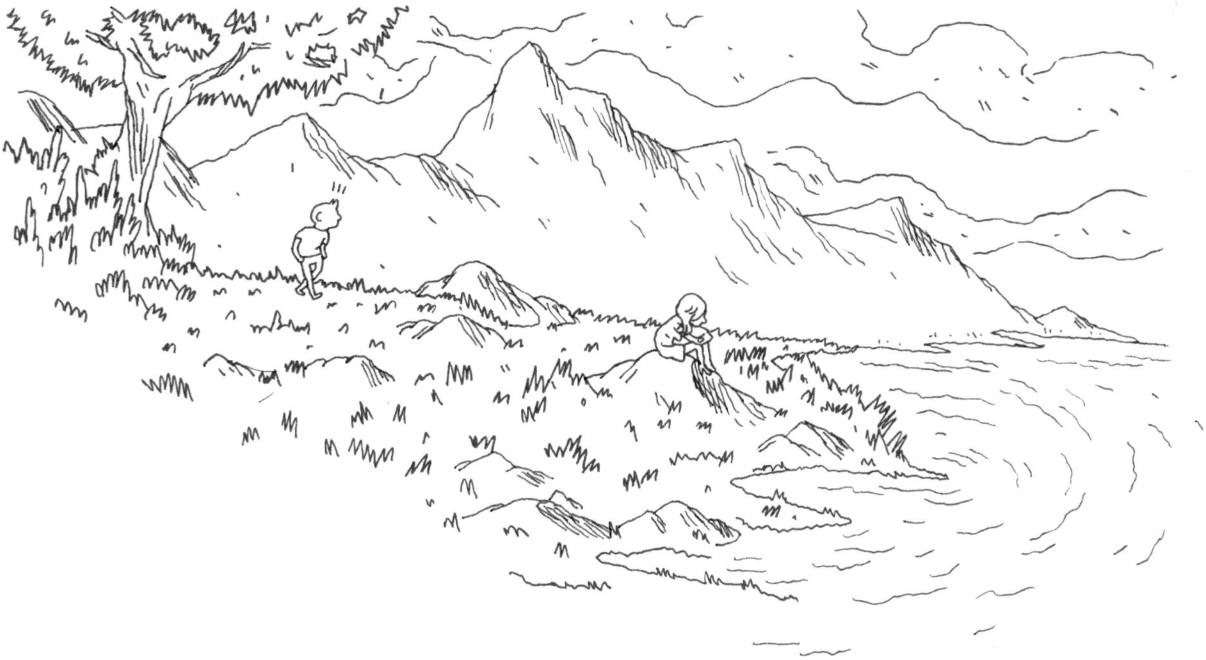

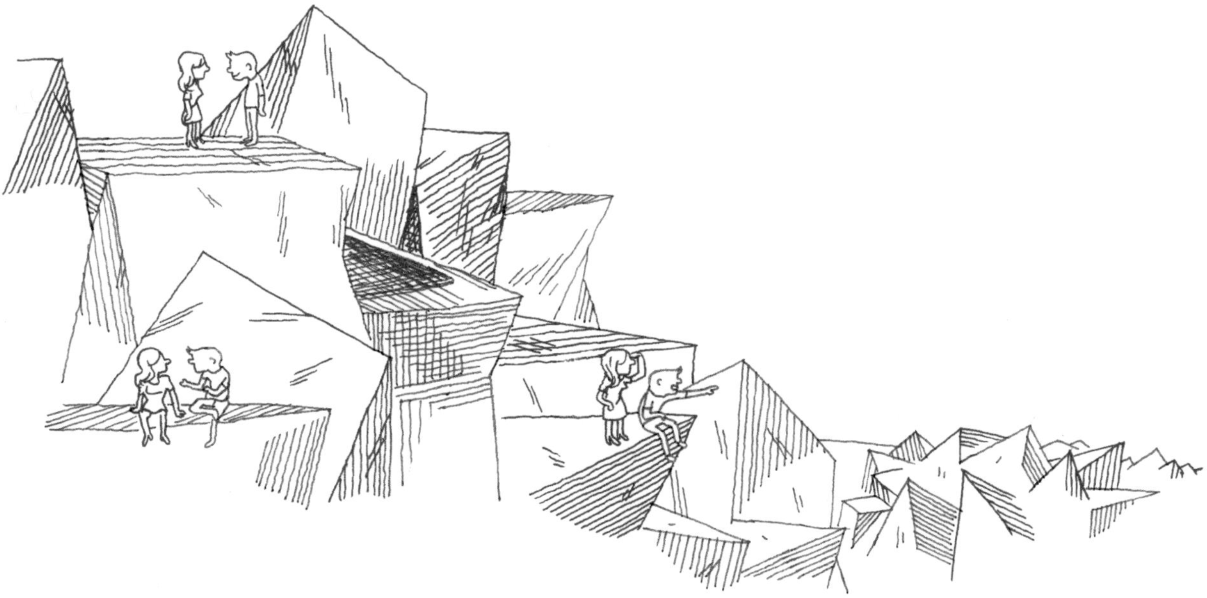

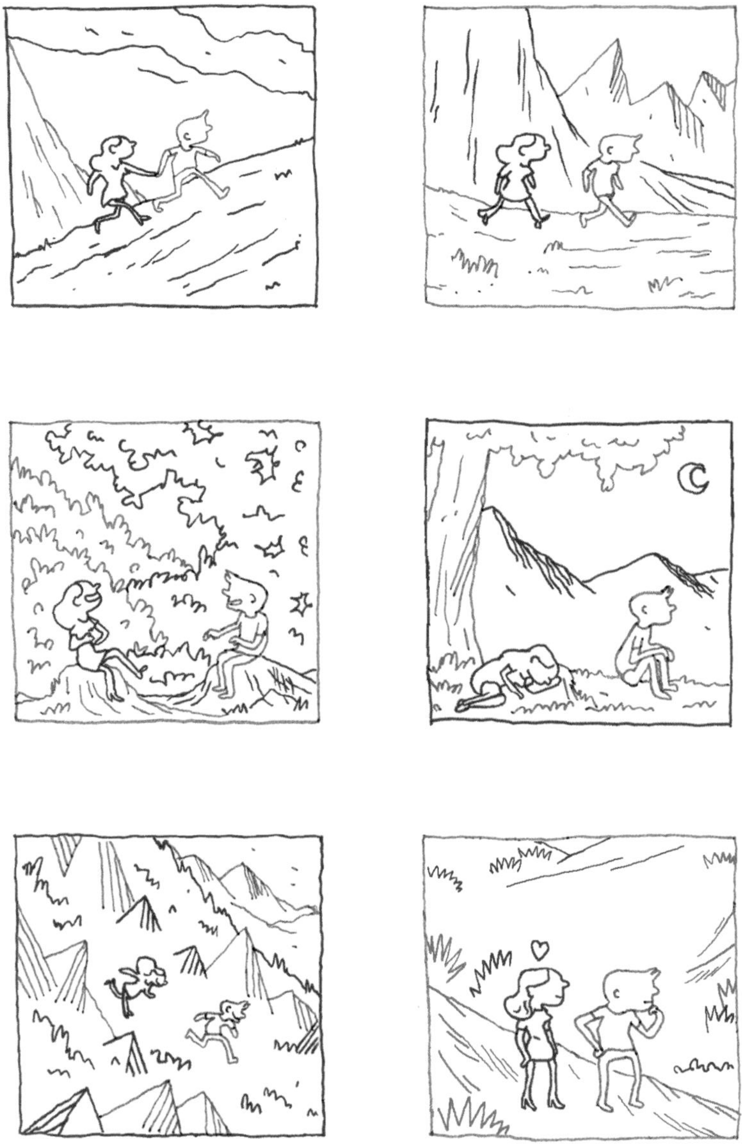

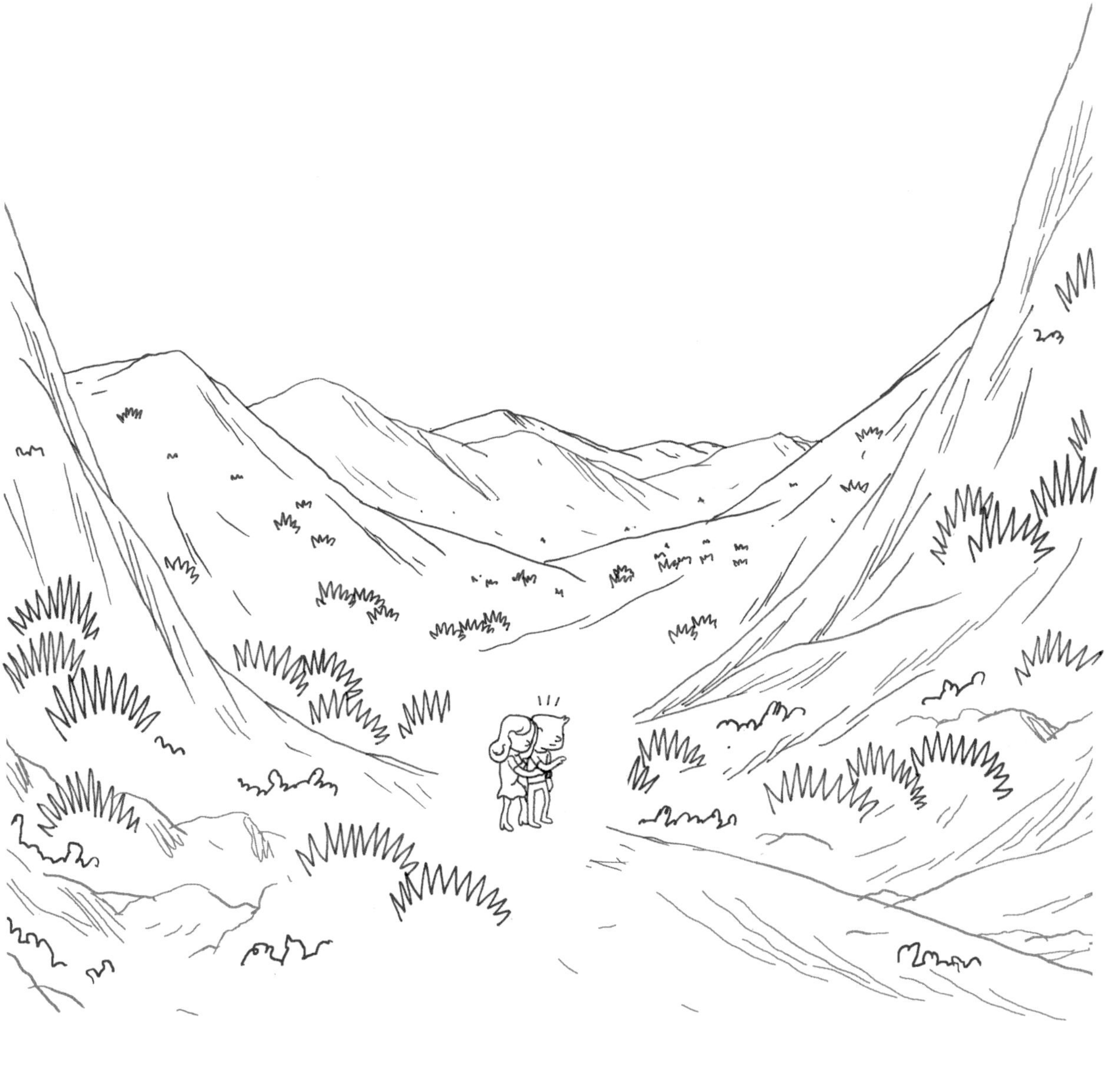

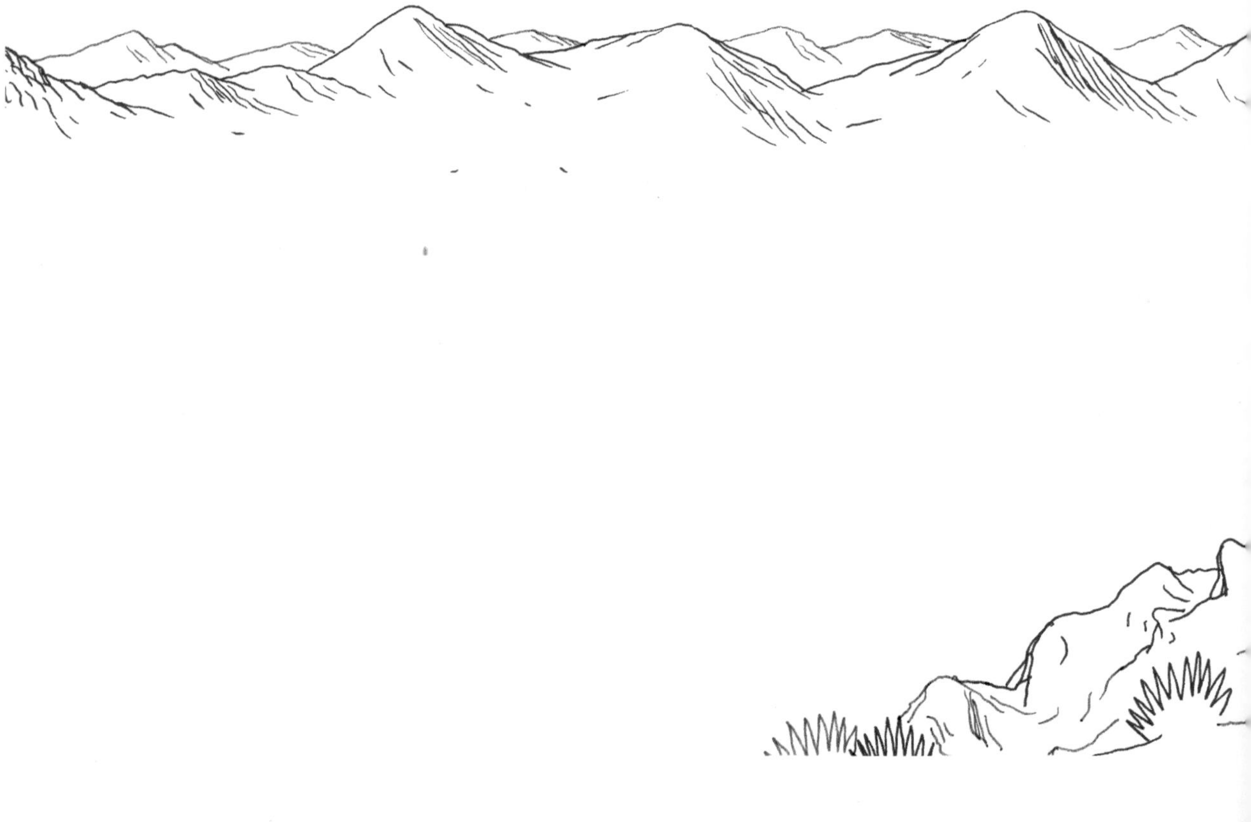

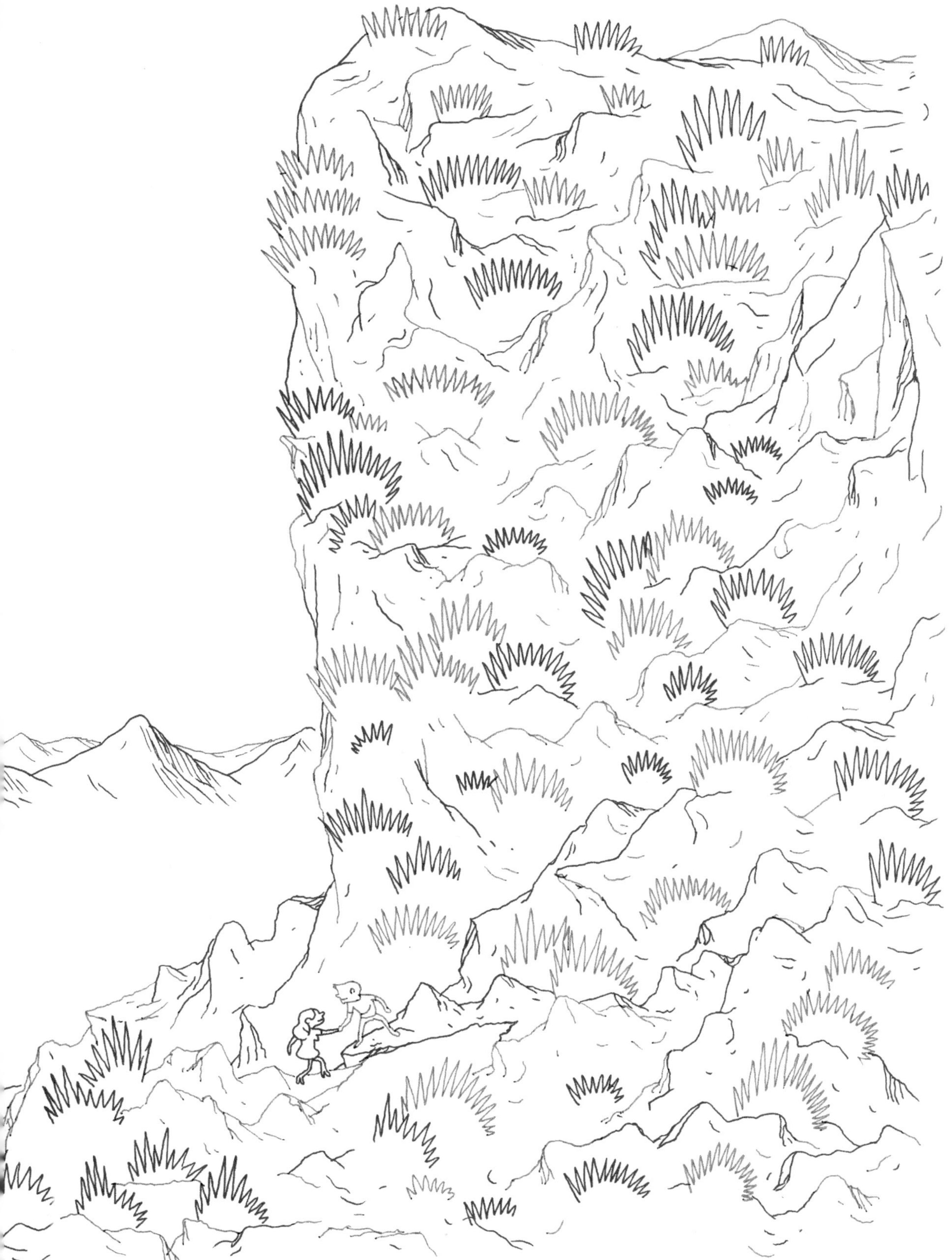

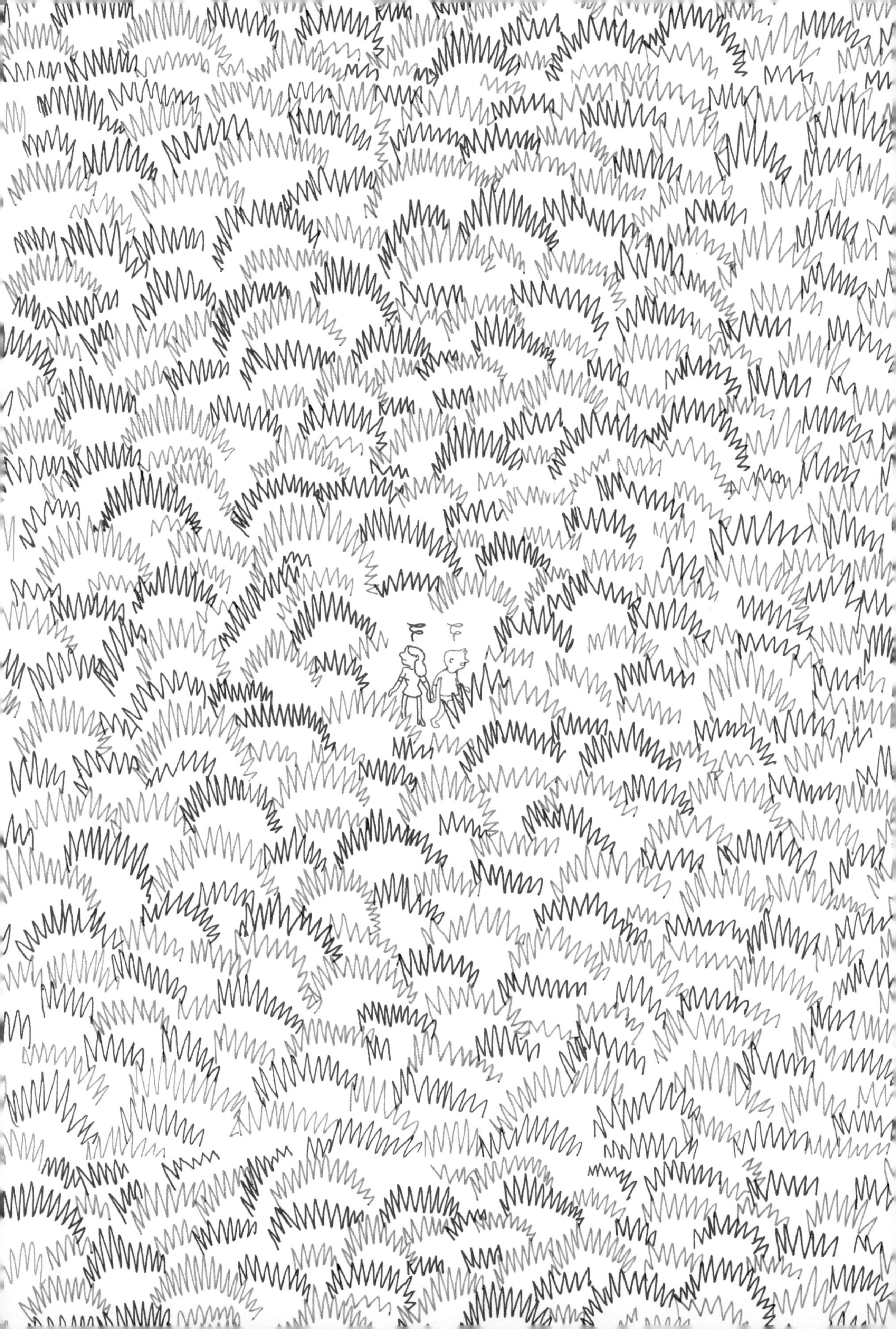

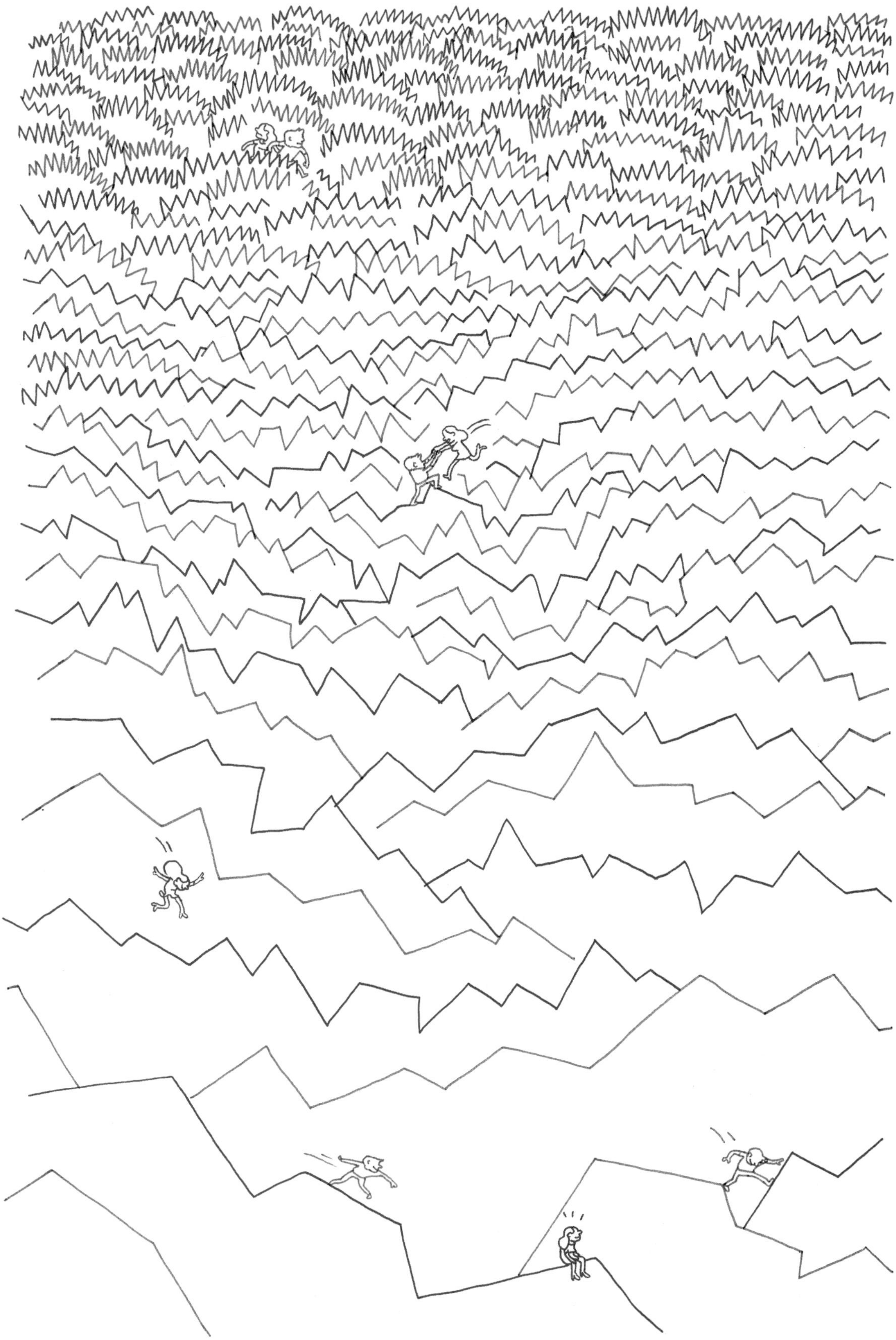

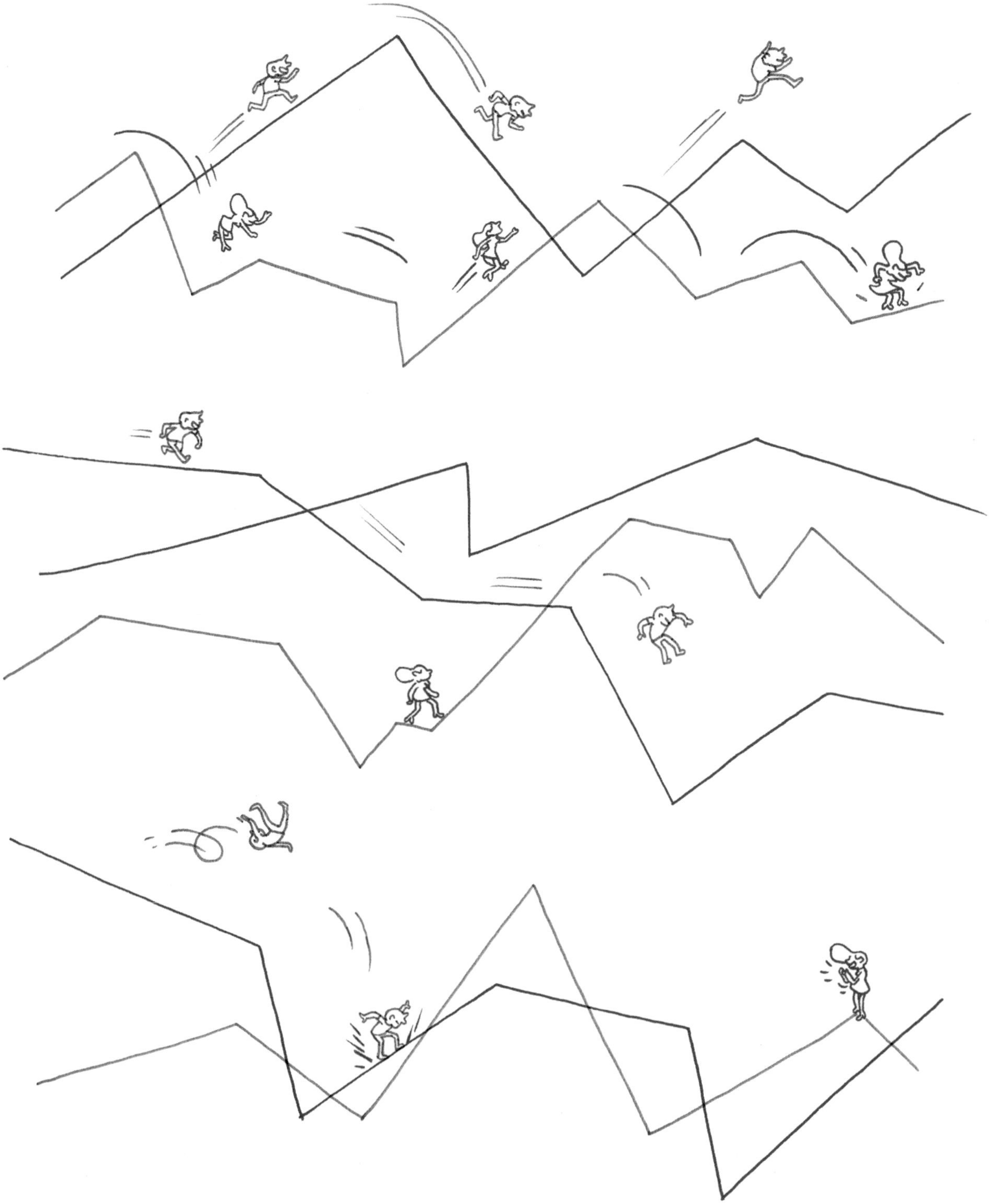

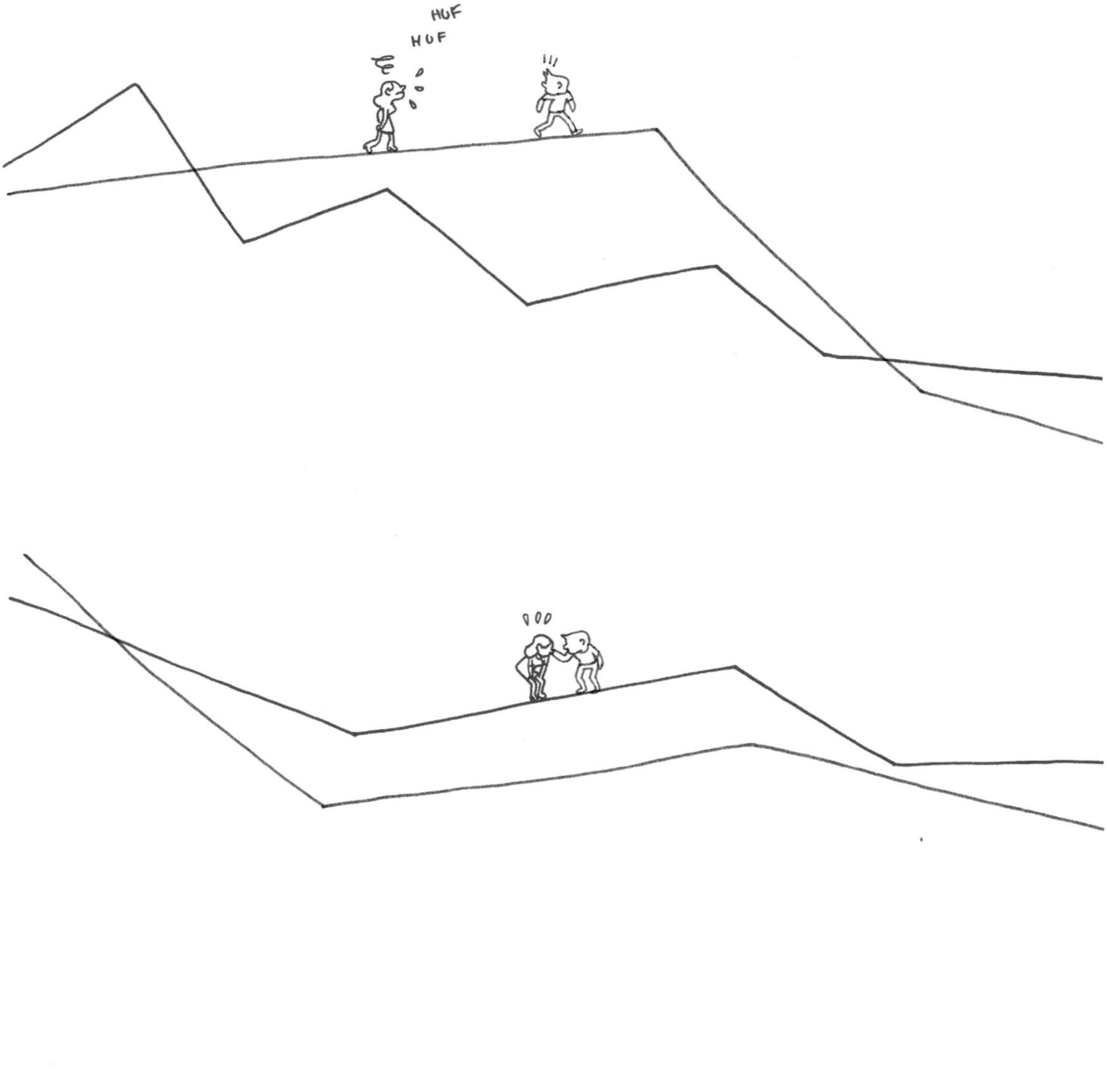
HUF
HUF

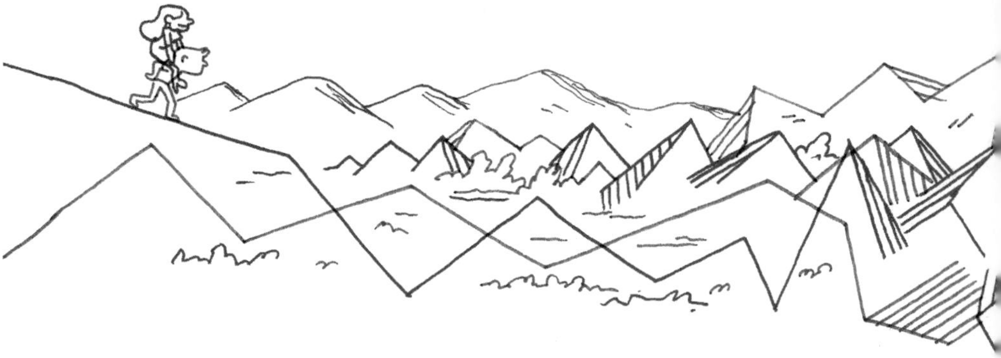

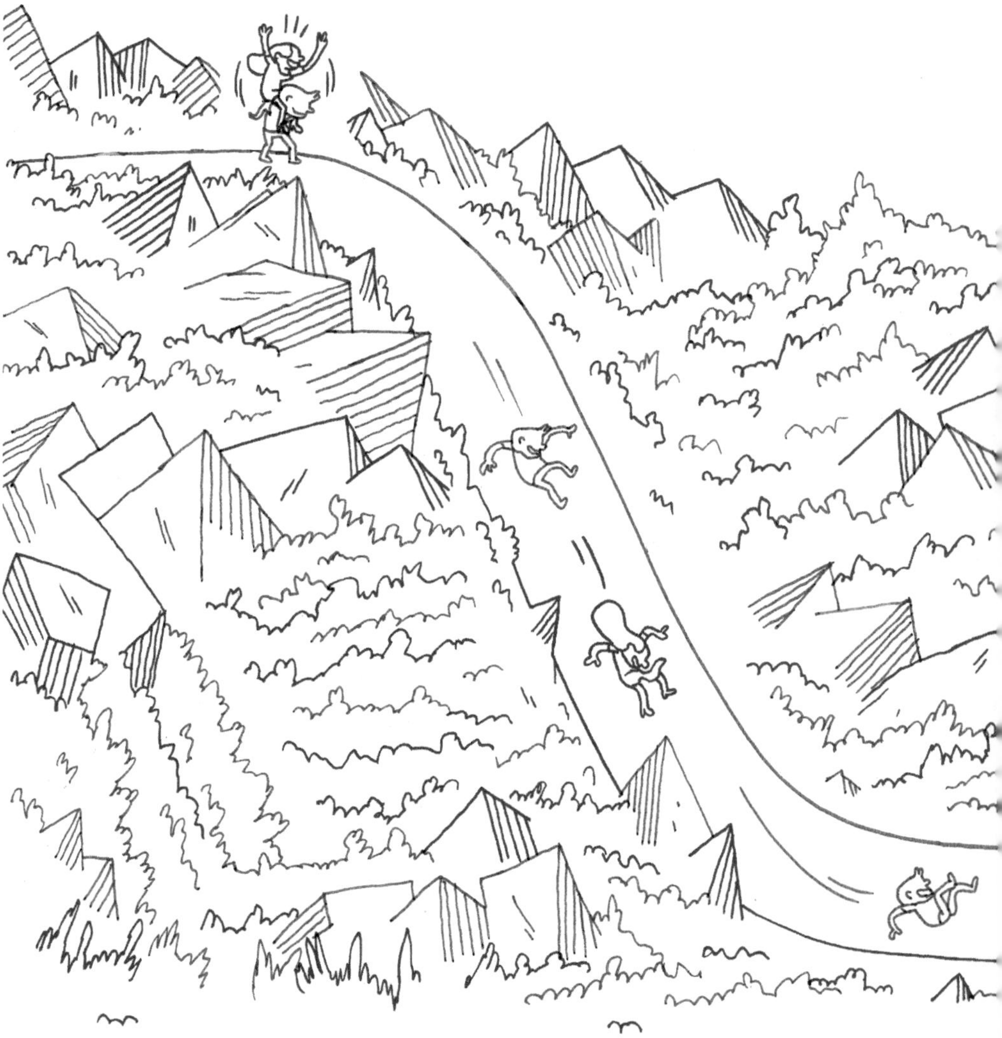

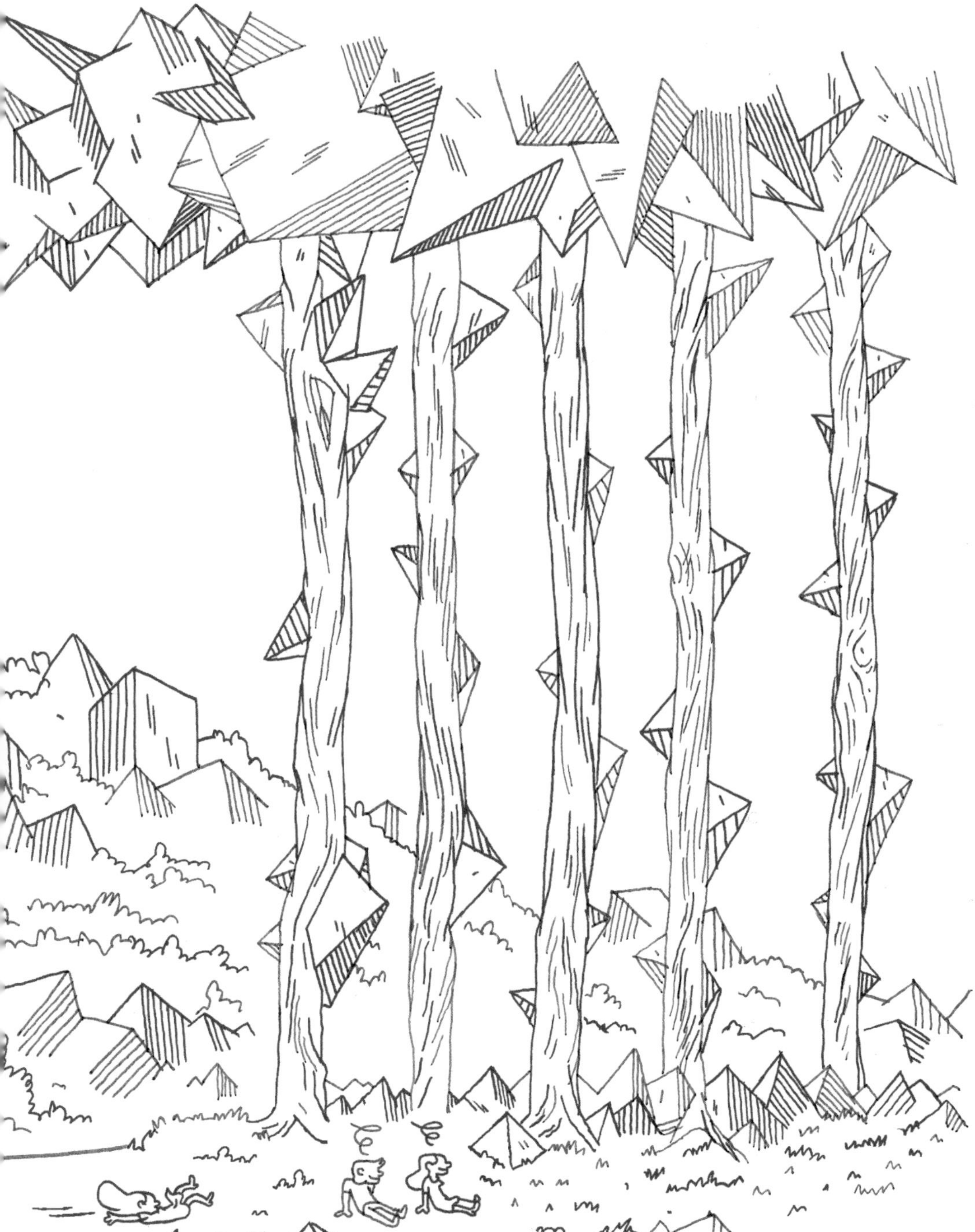

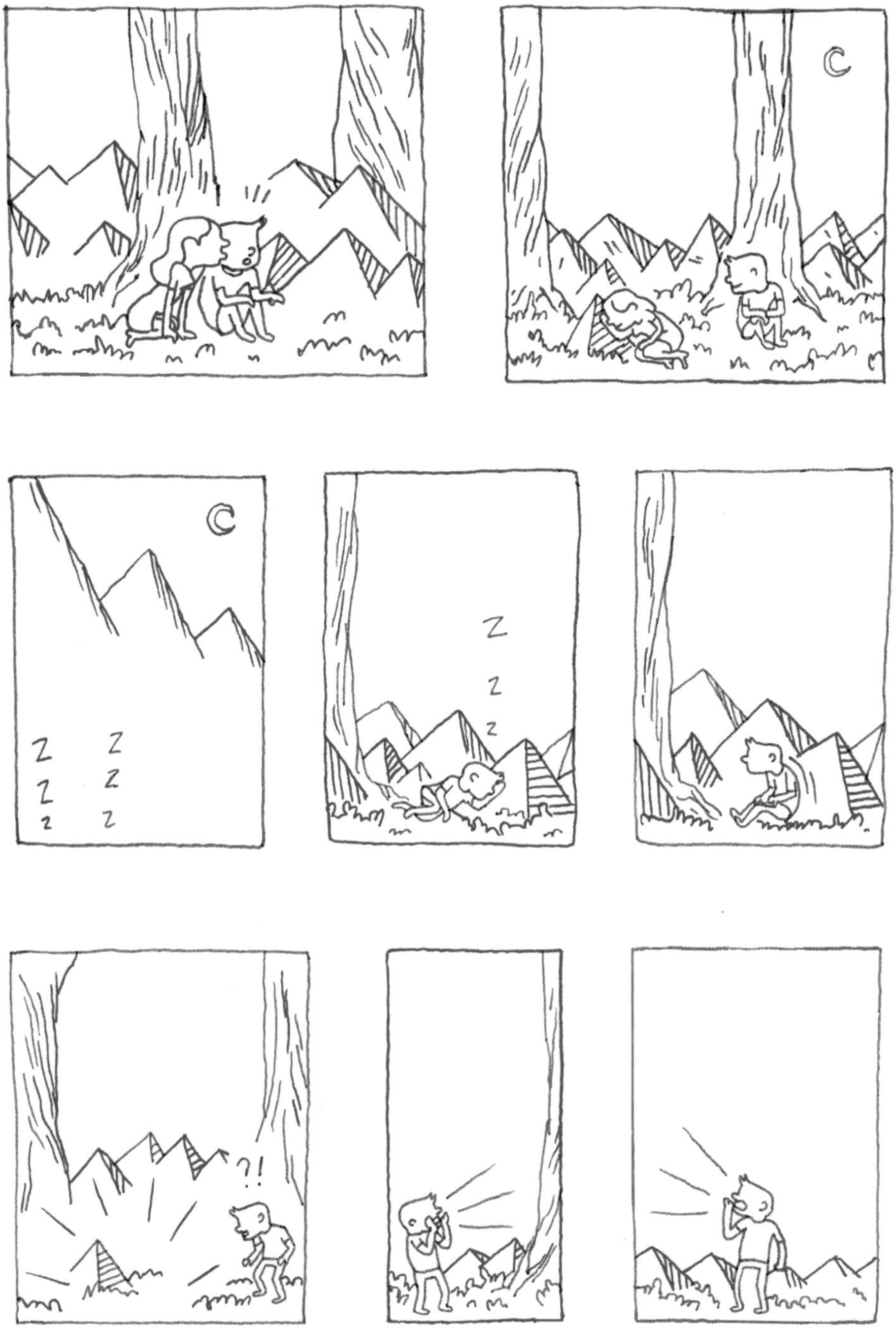
Z Z z
Z Z z
Z Z z
?!

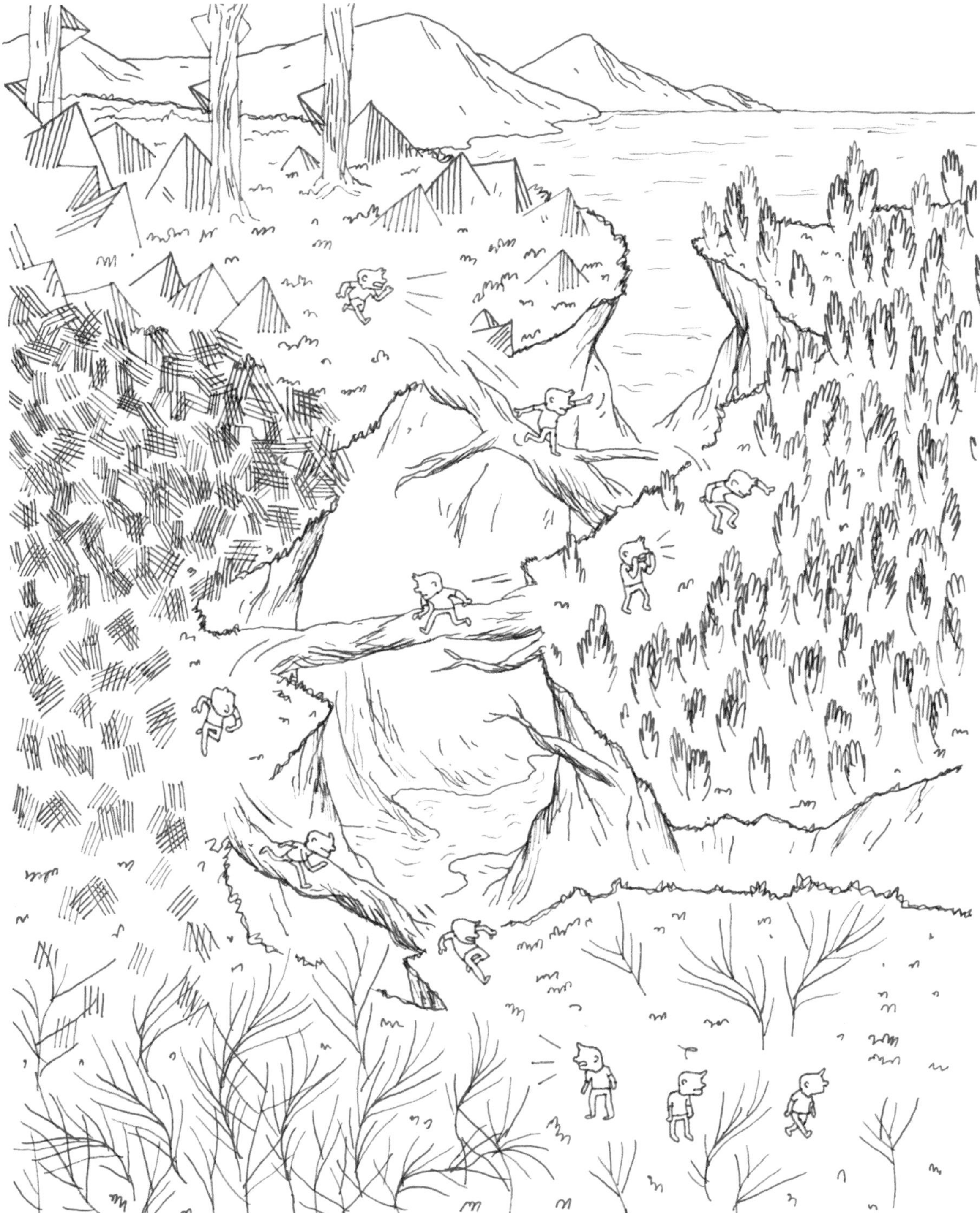

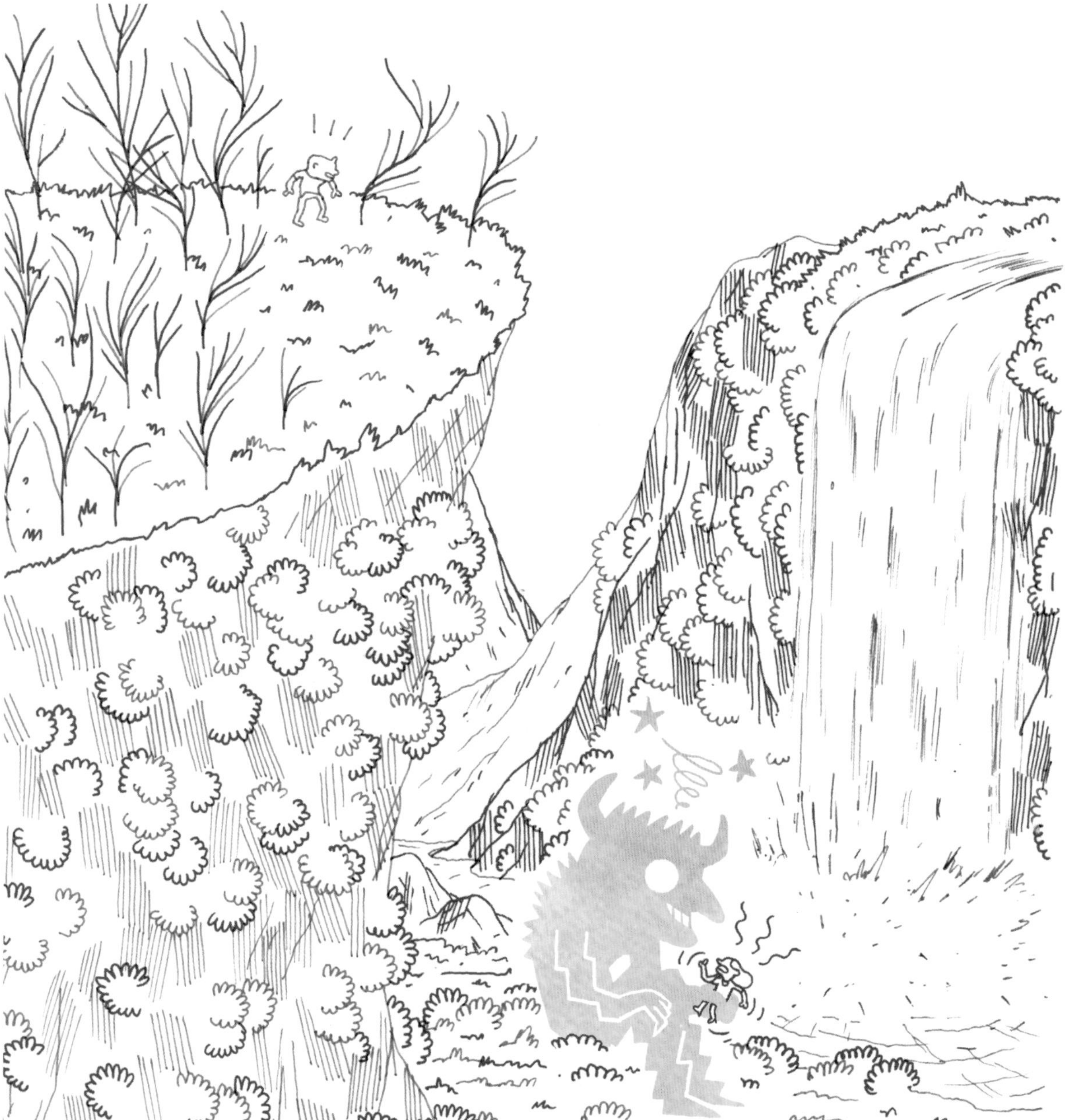

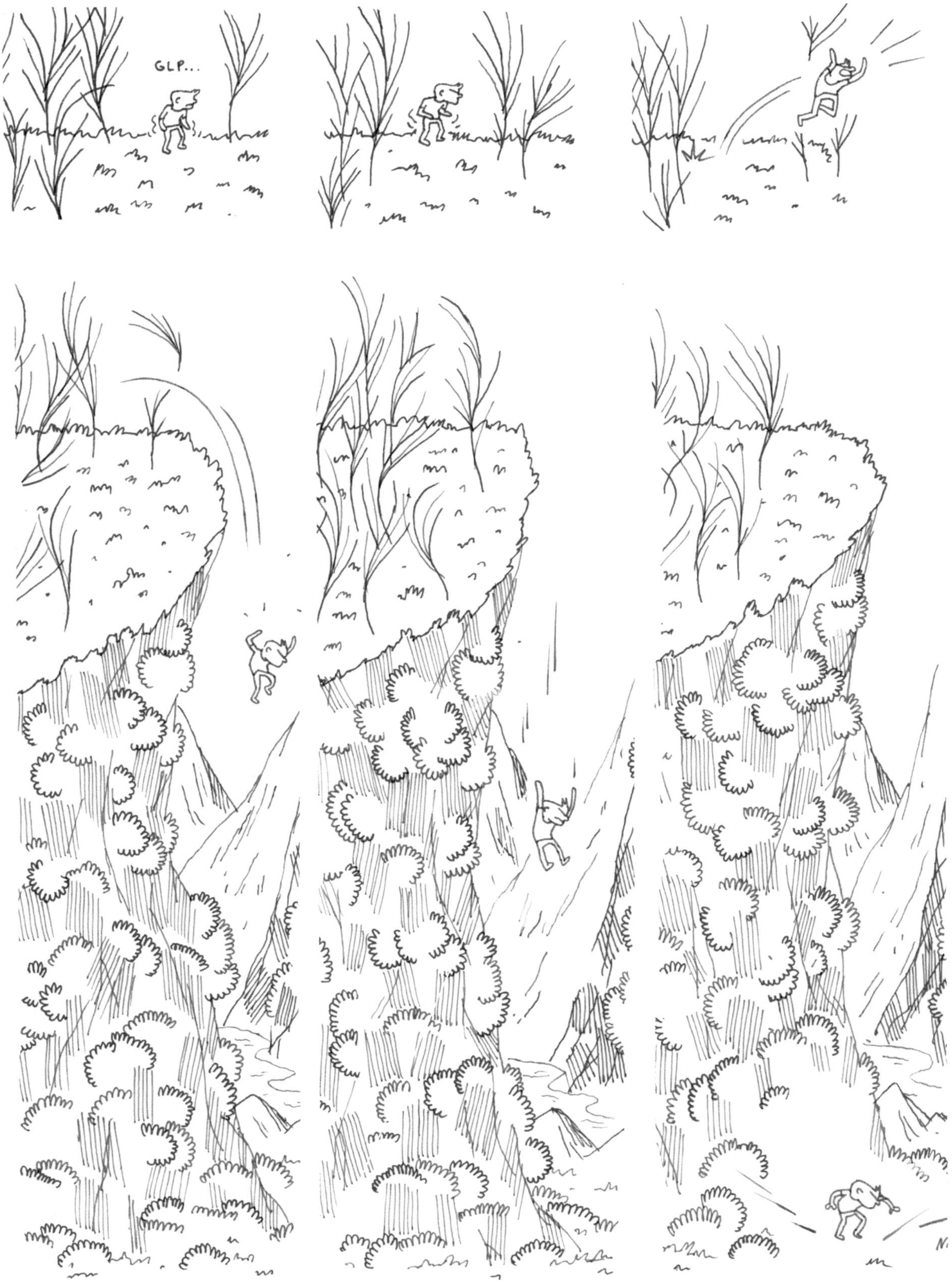
GLP...

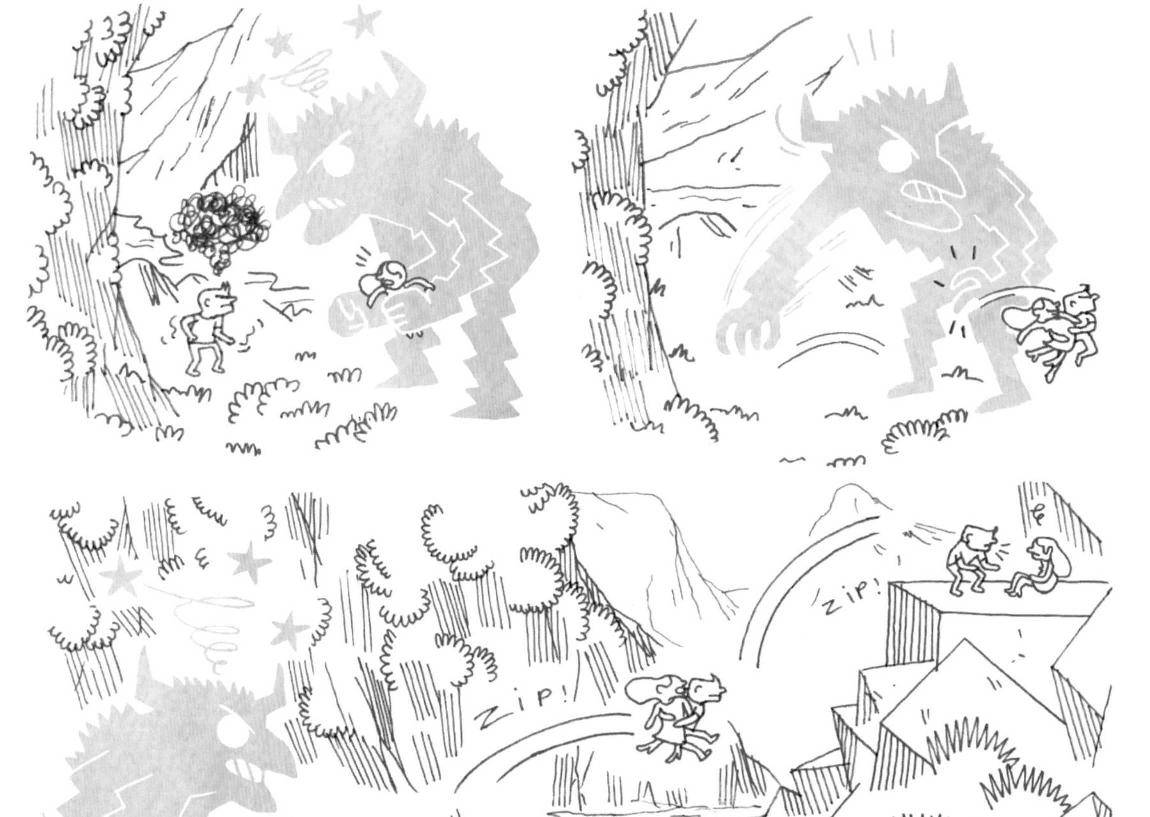
ZIP!
ZIP!

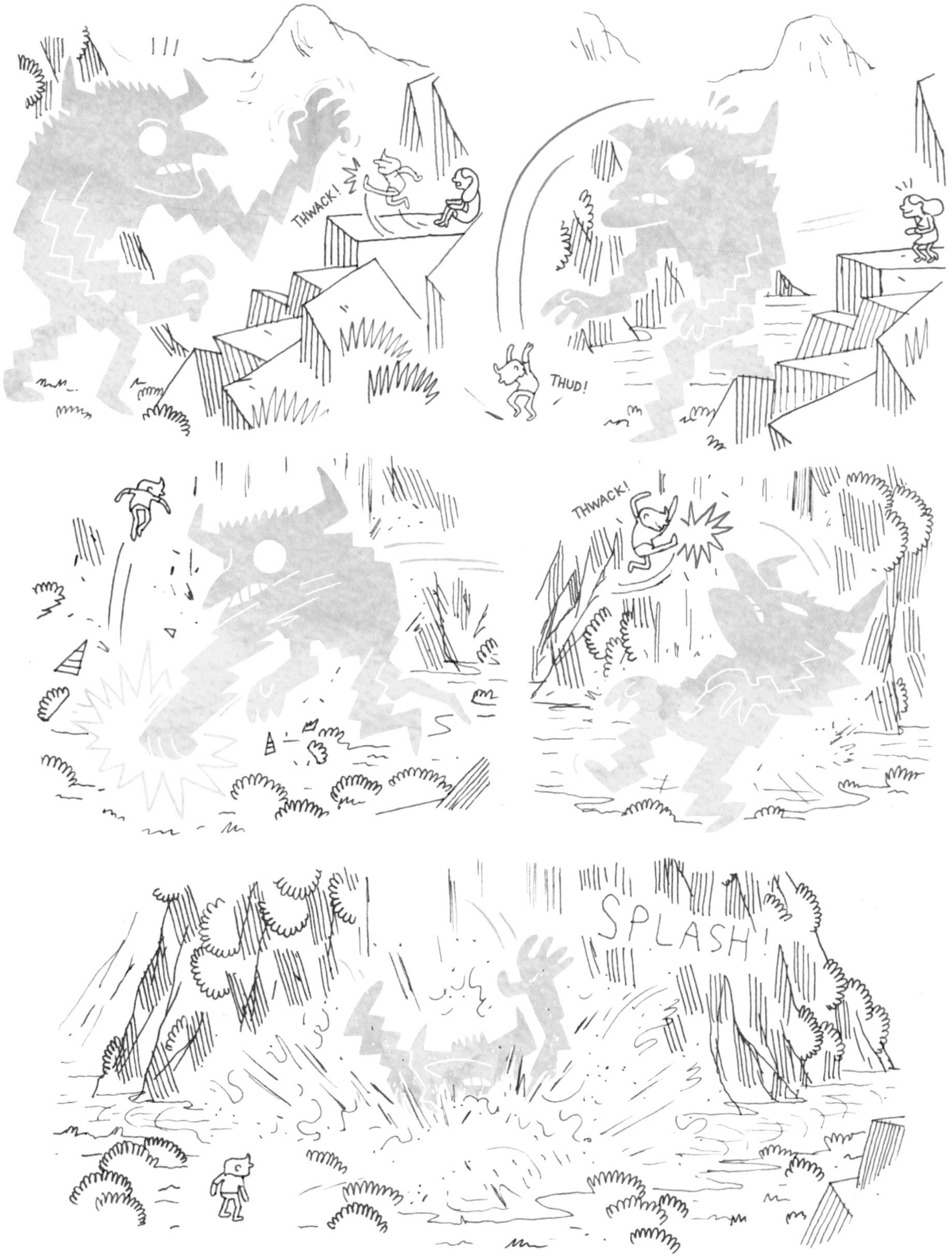
THWACK!
THUD!
THWACK!
SPLASH!

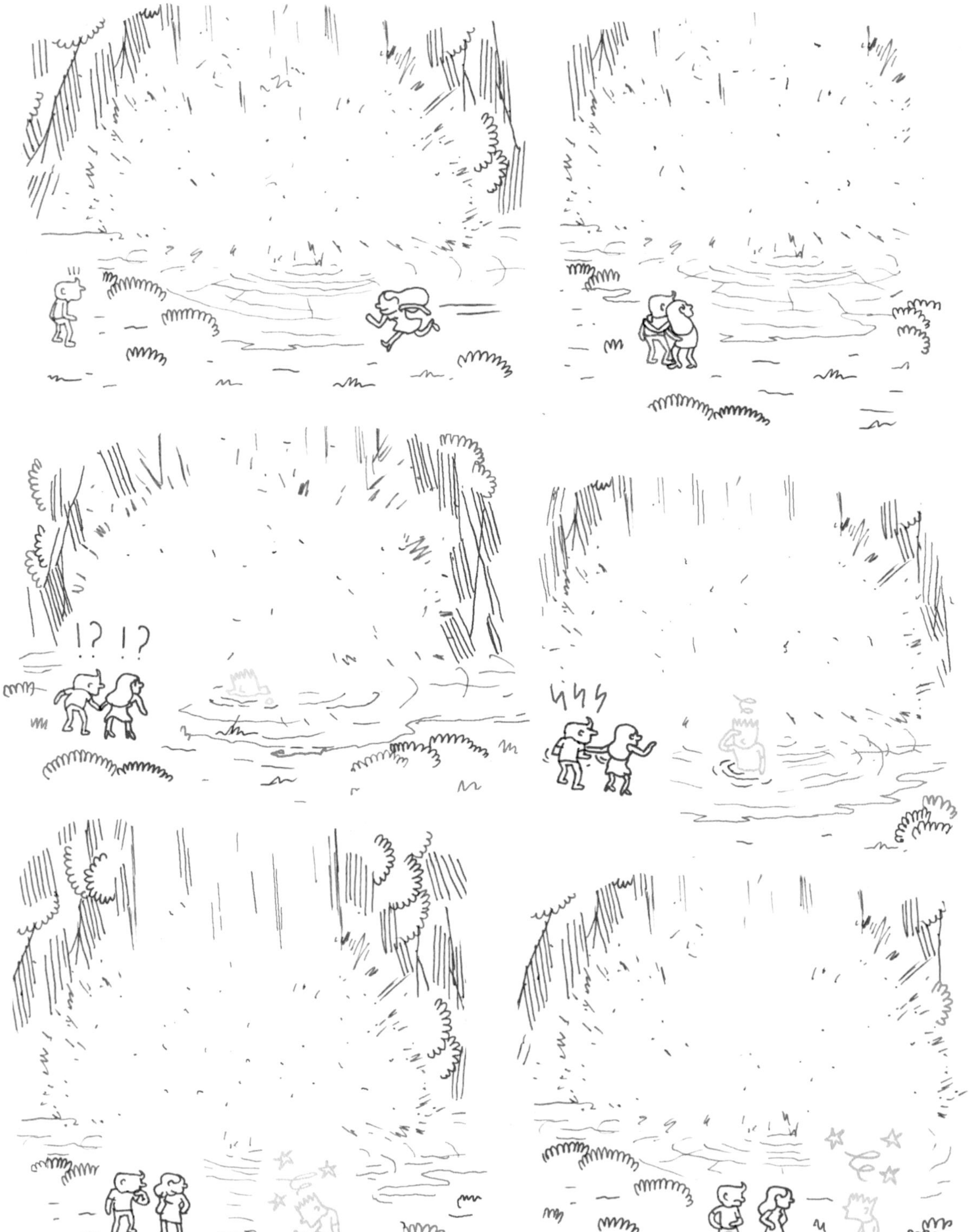

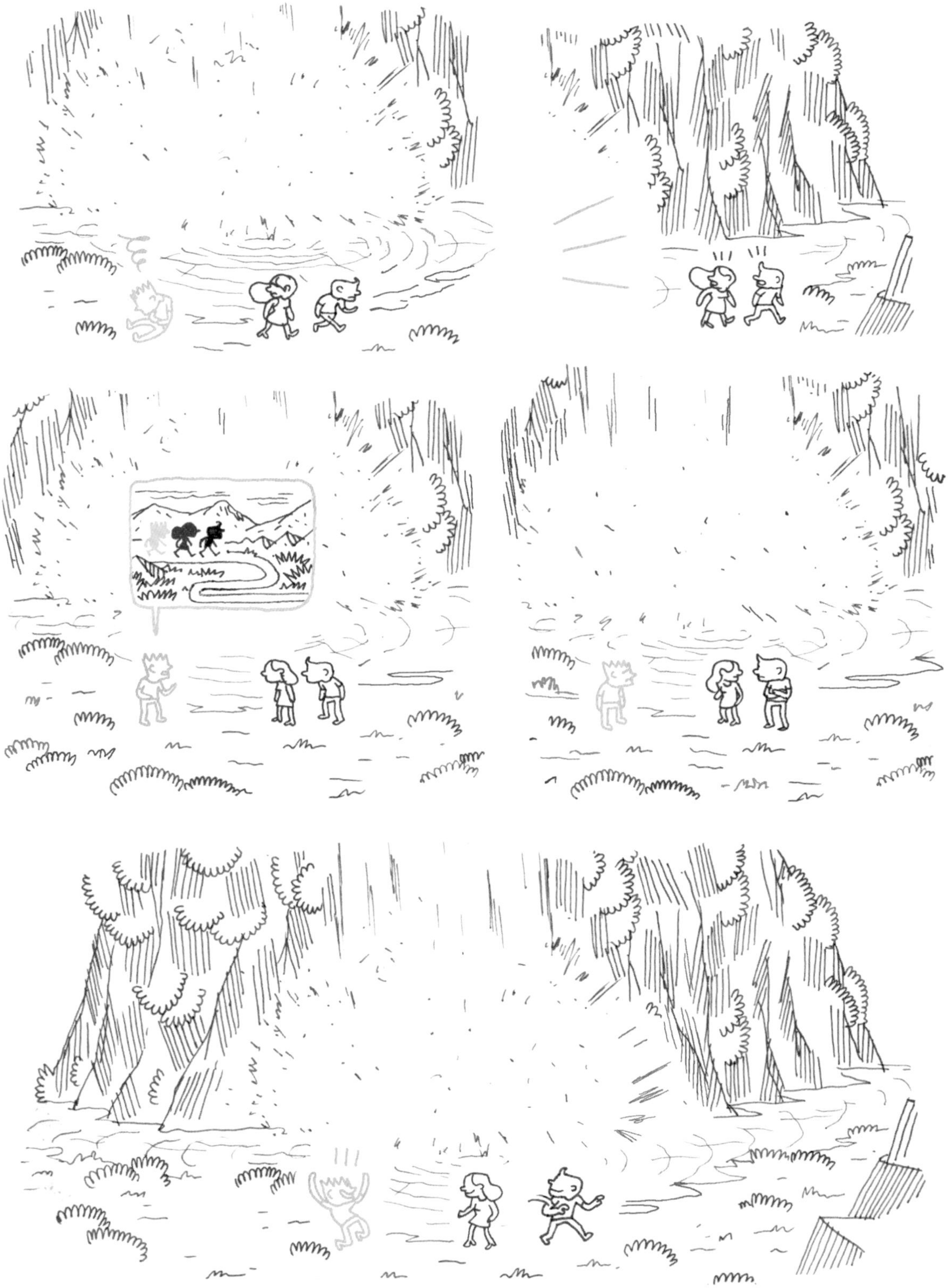

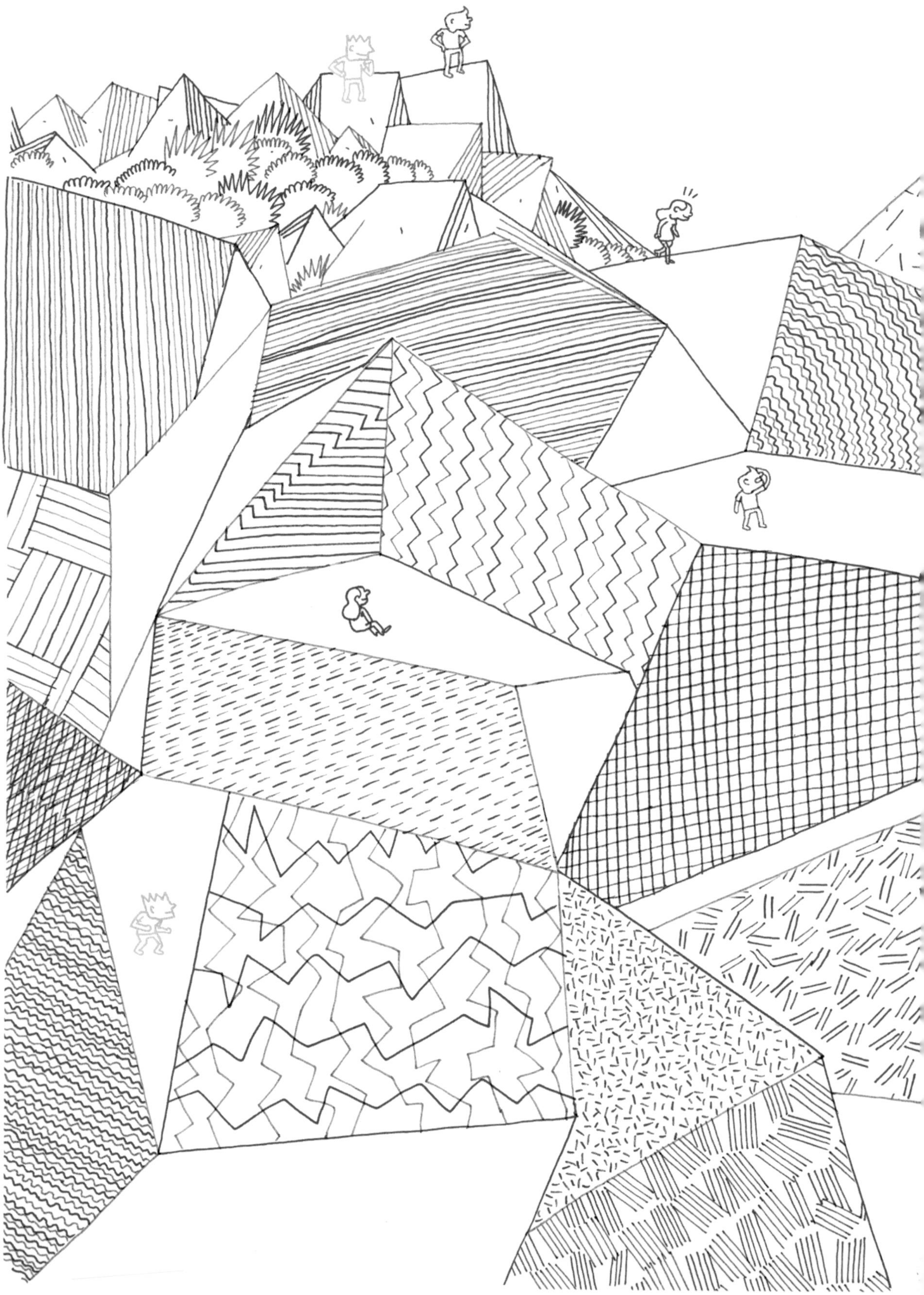

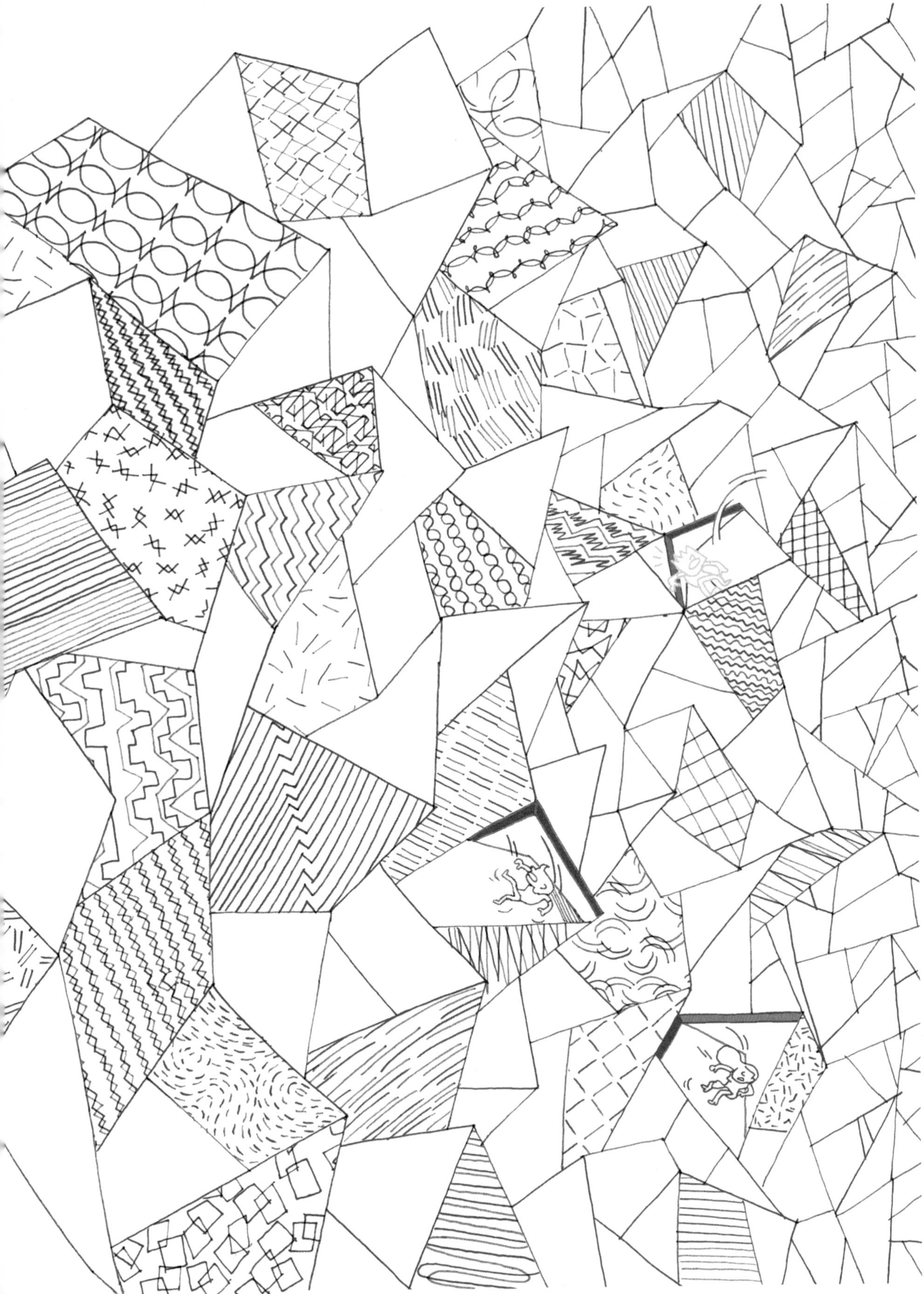

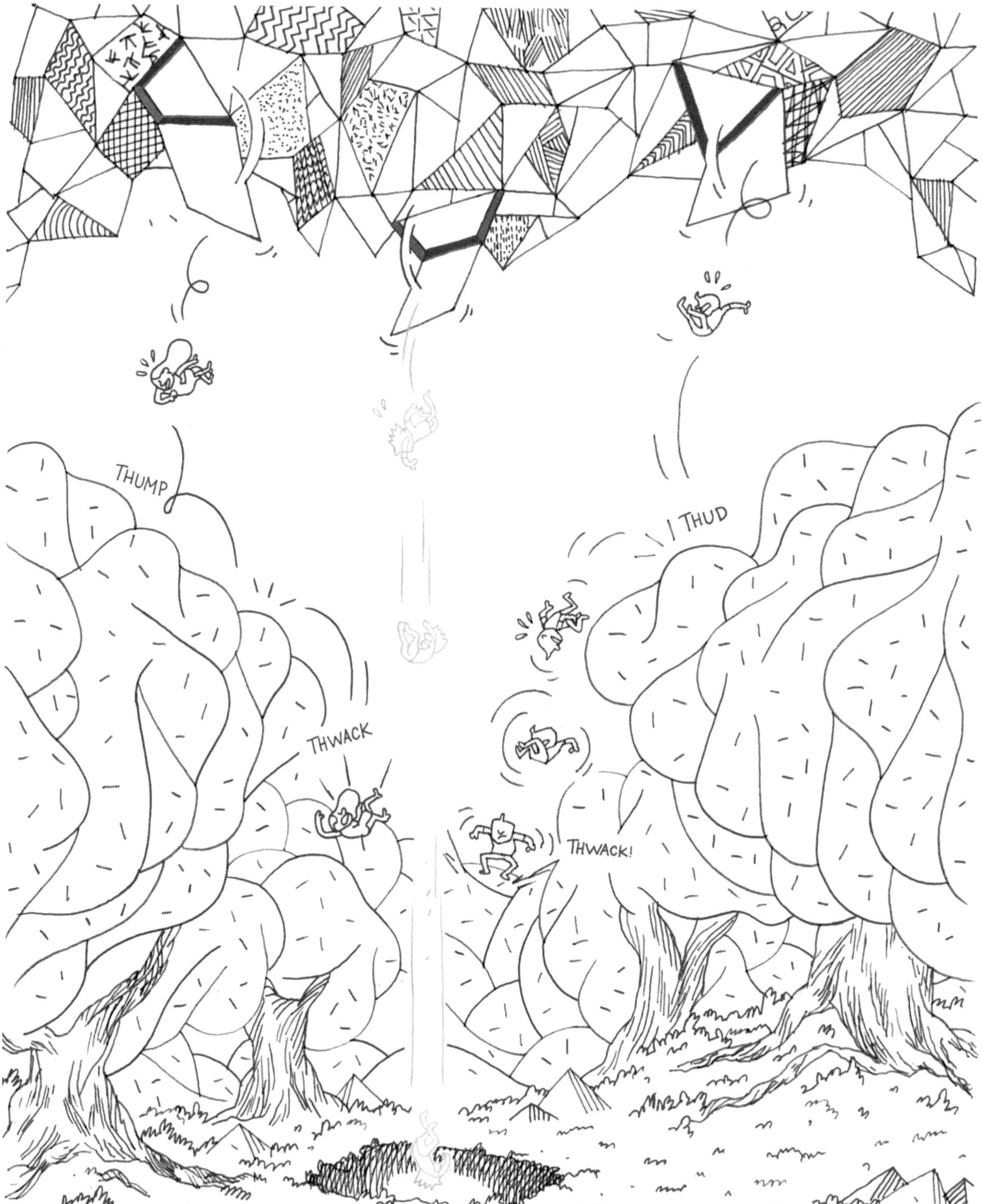
THUMP
THUD
THWACK
THWACK!

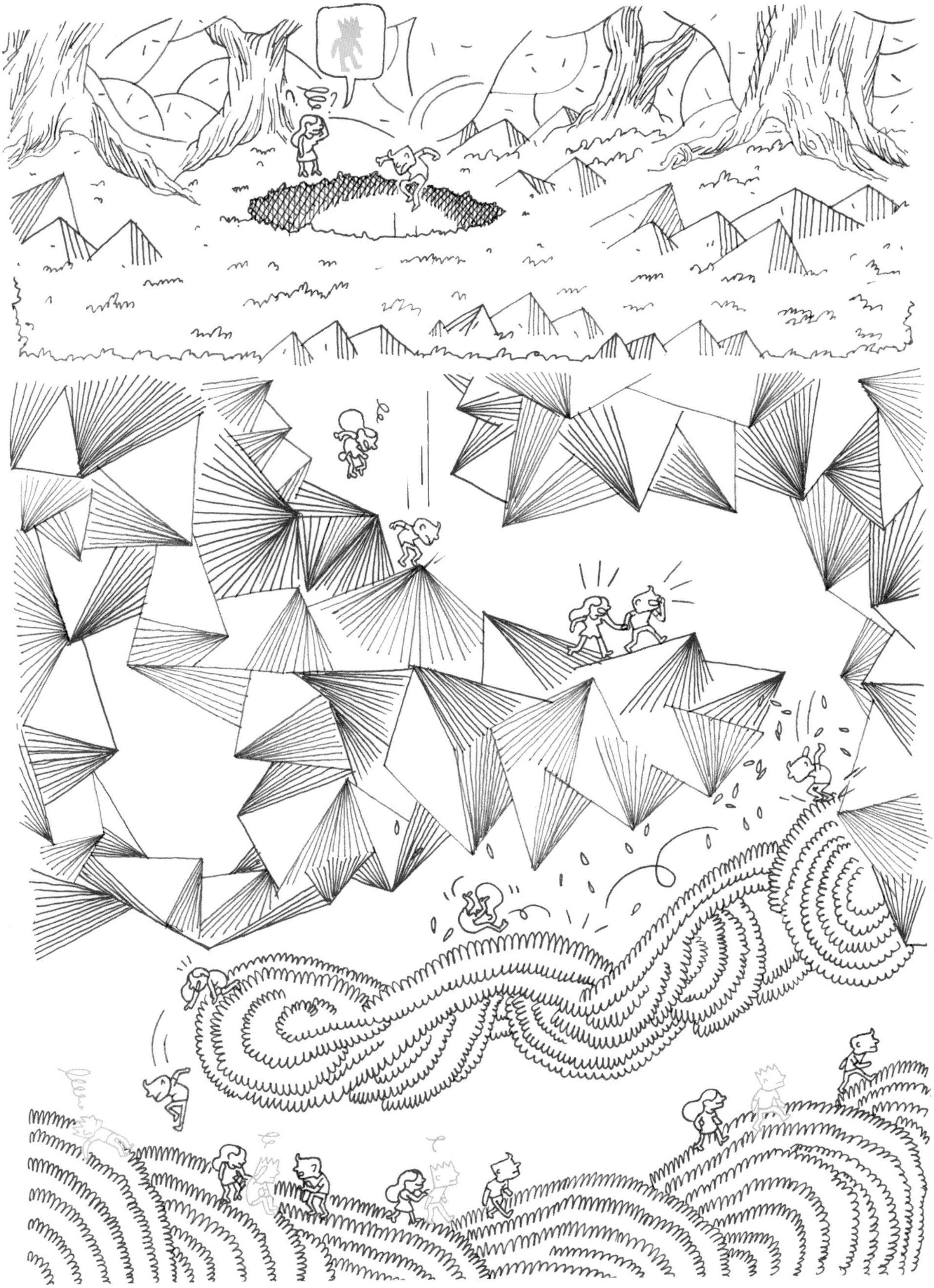

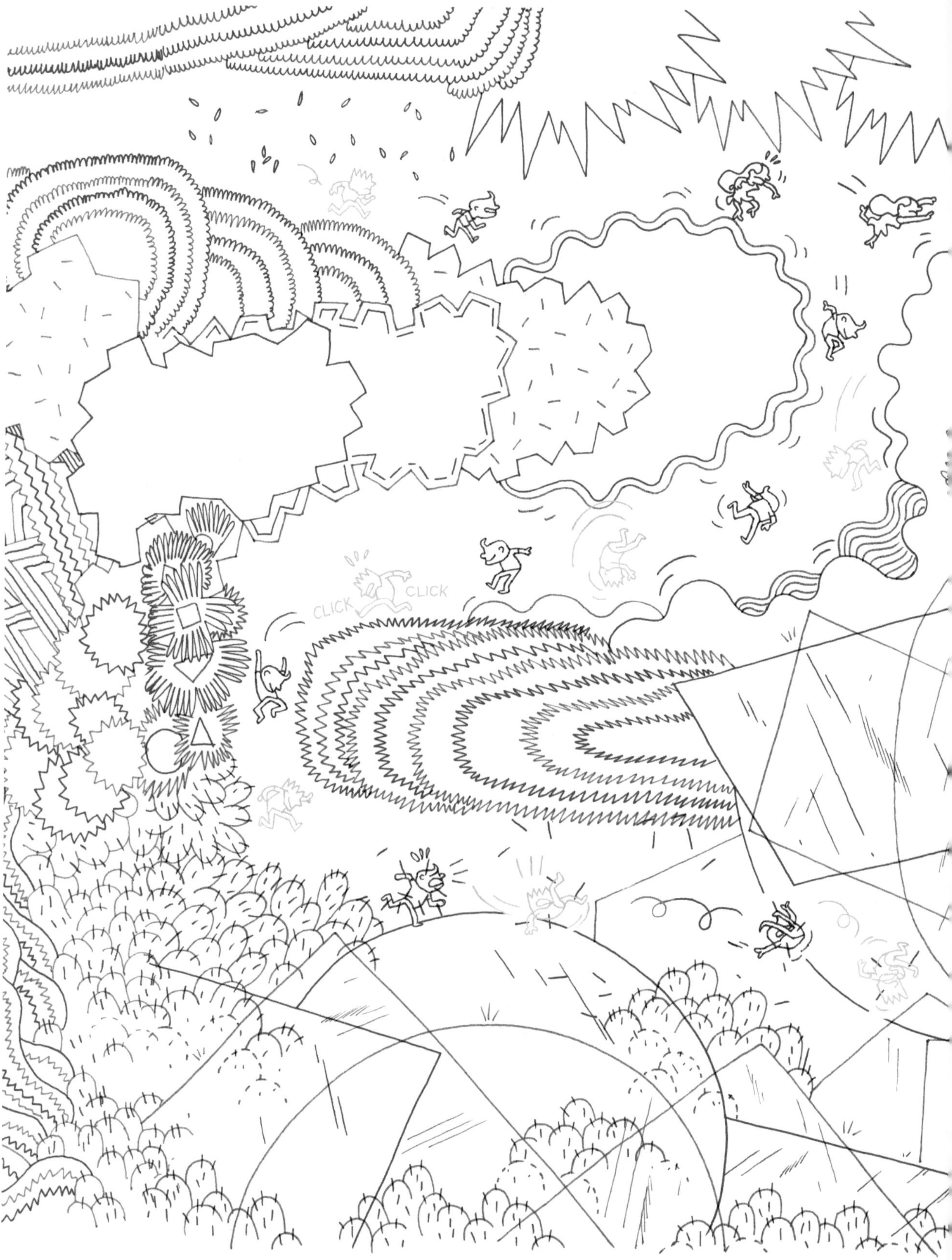
CLICK
CLICK

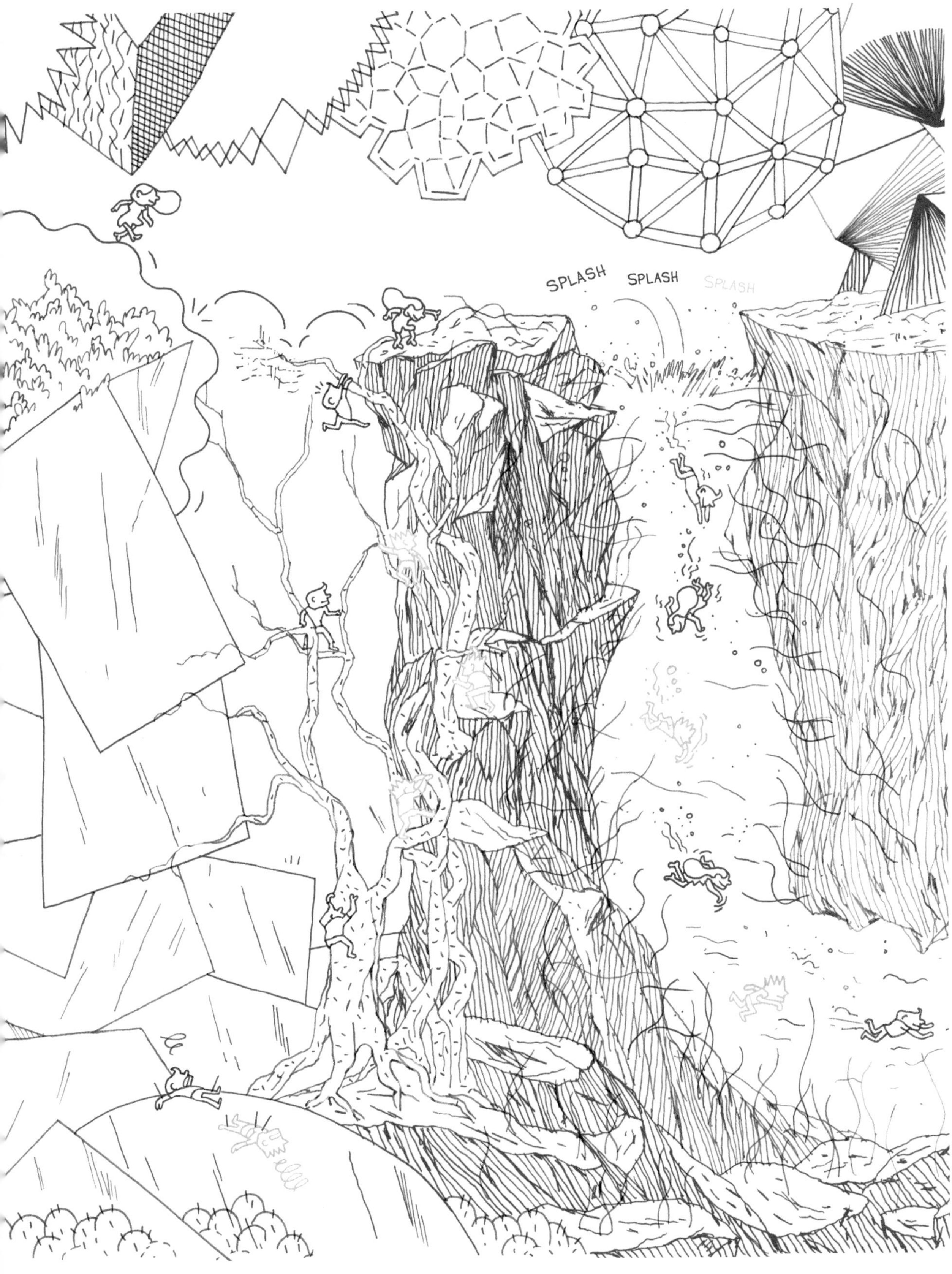
SPLASH
SPLASH
SPLASH

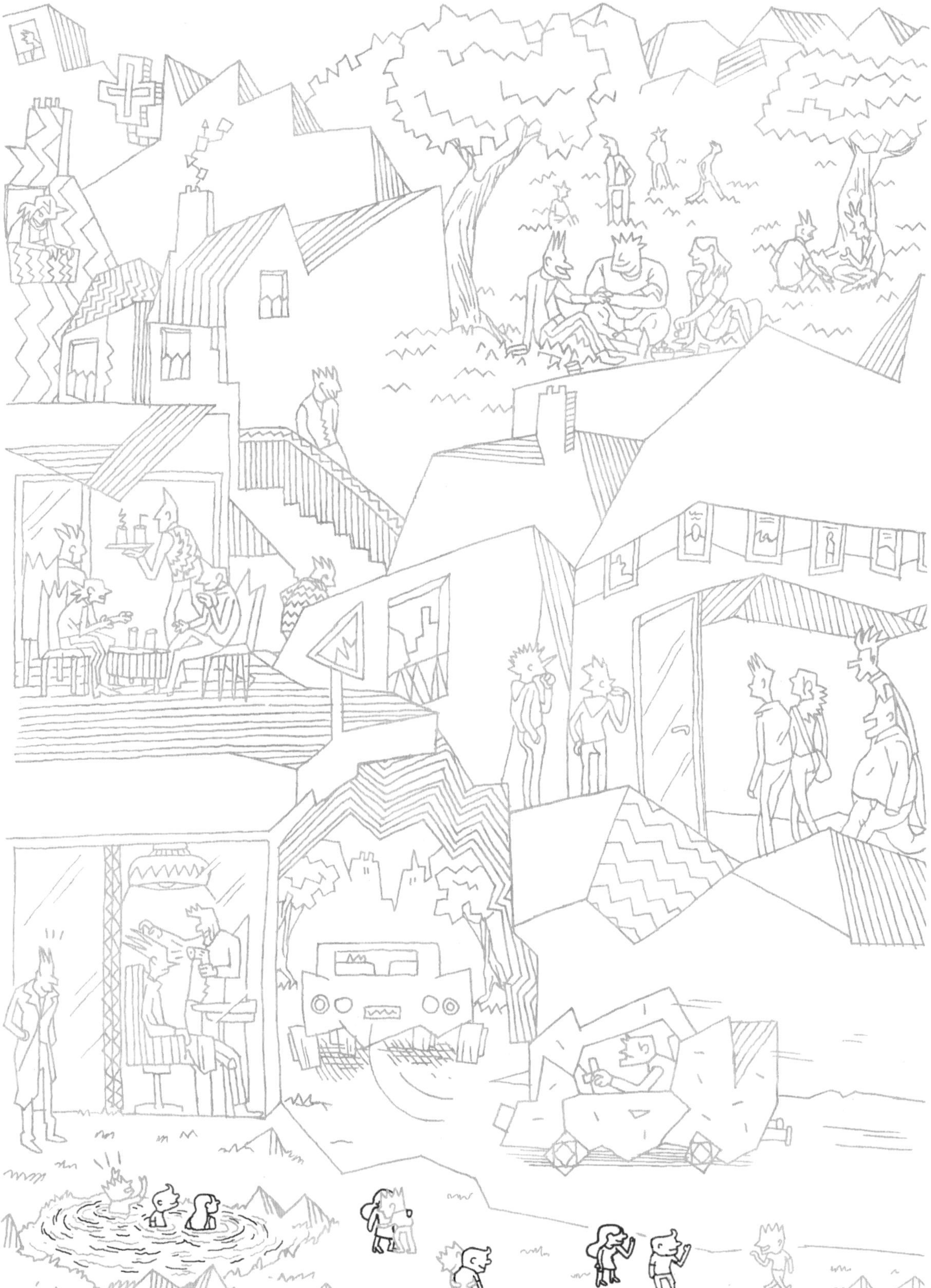

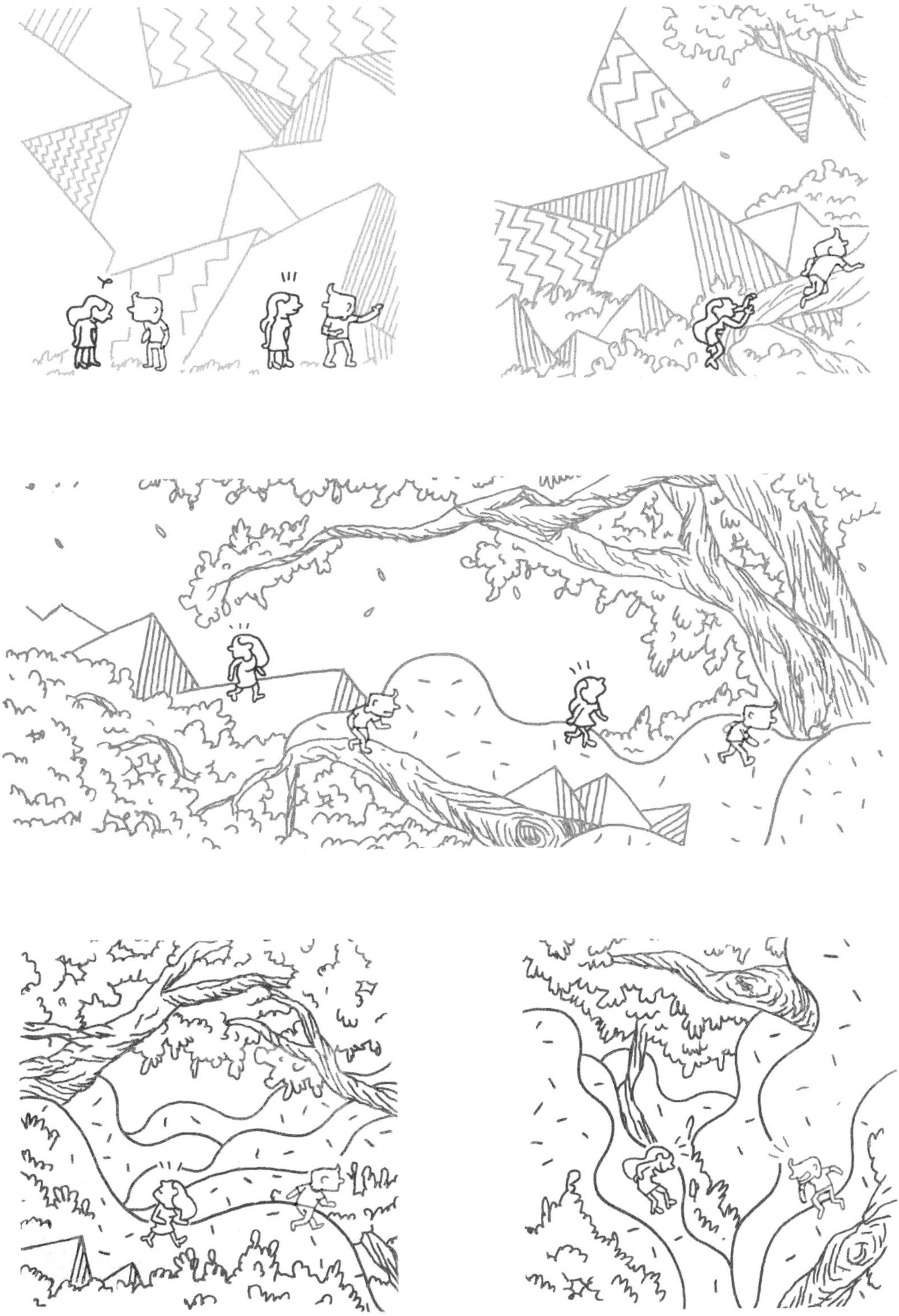

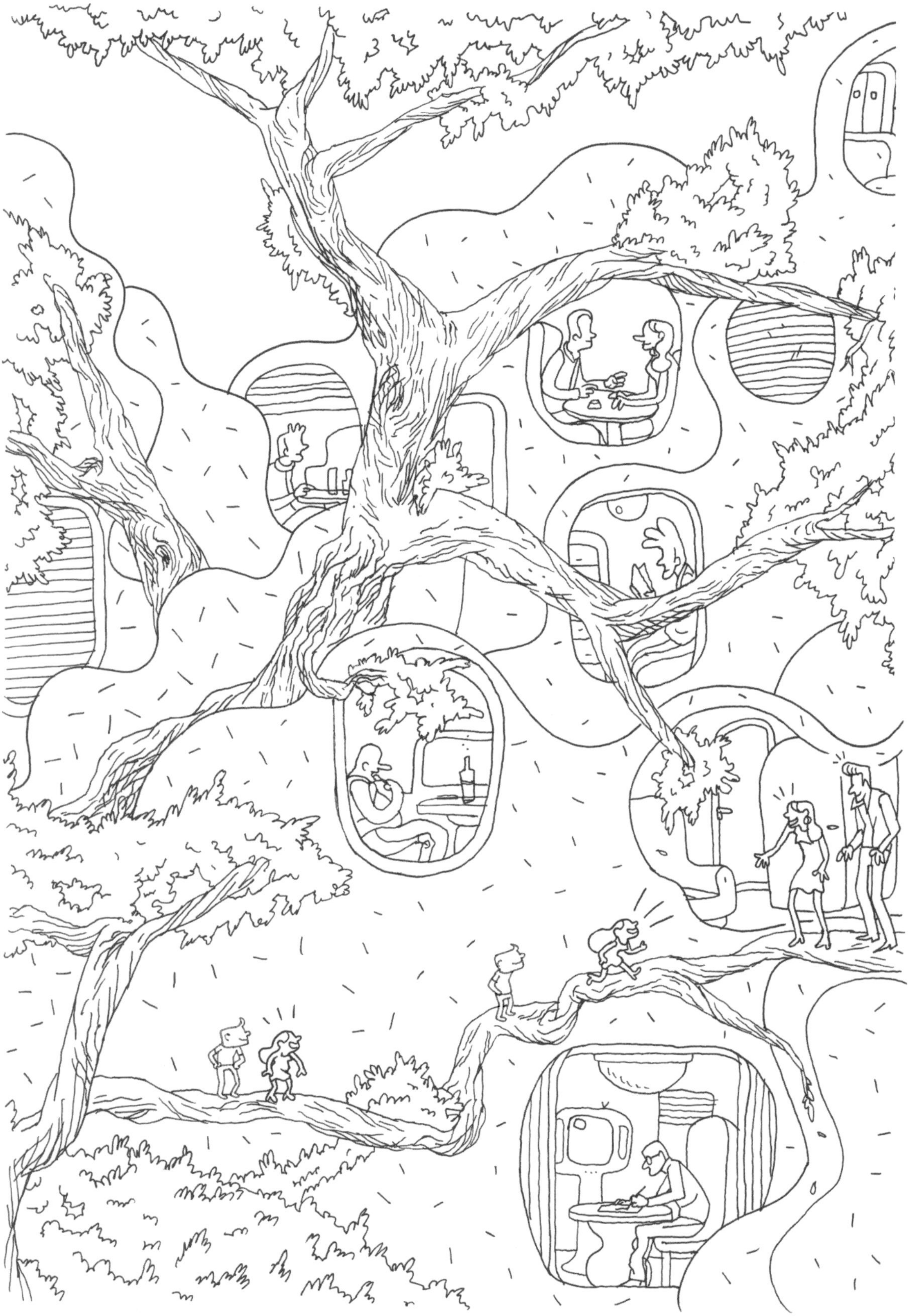

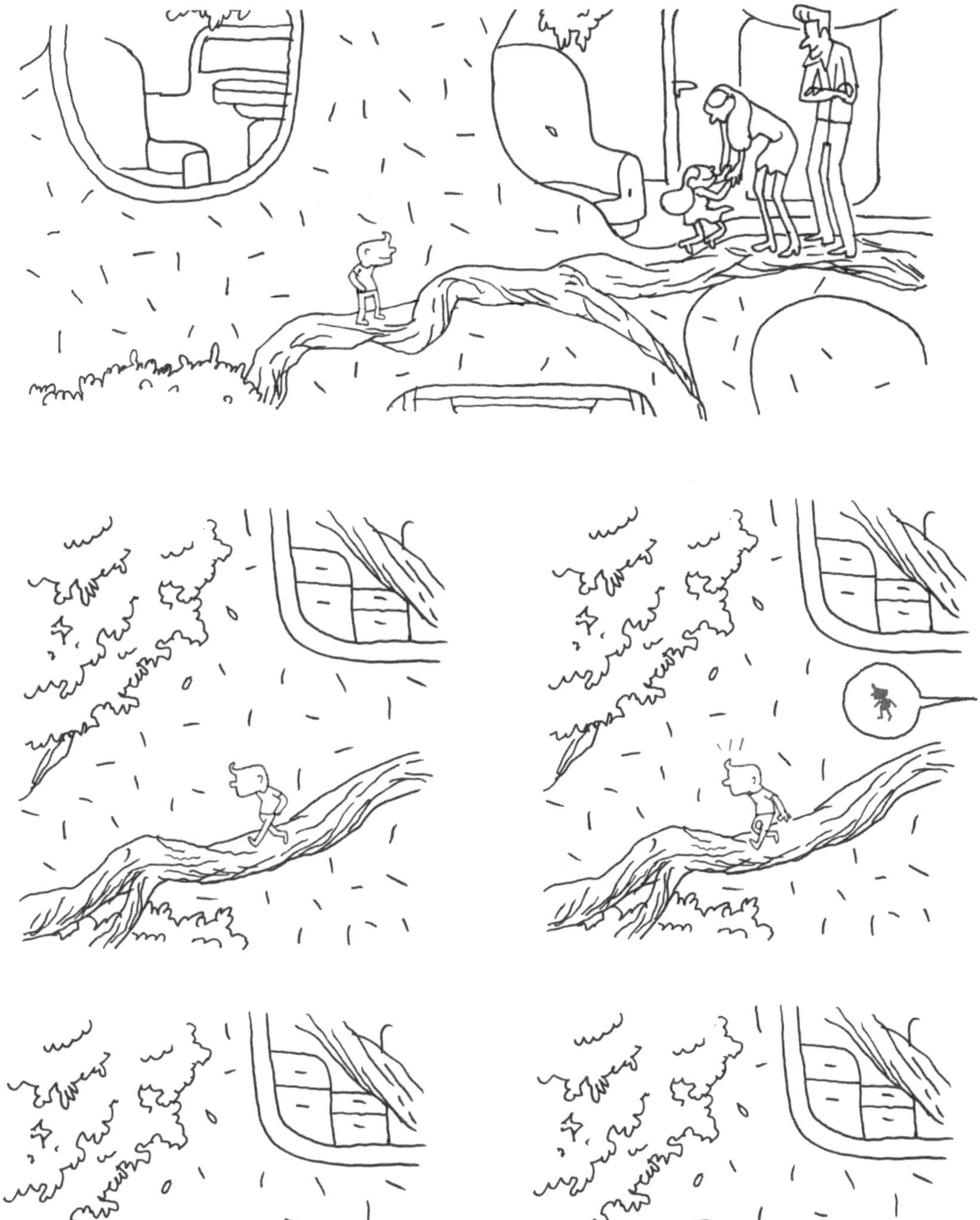

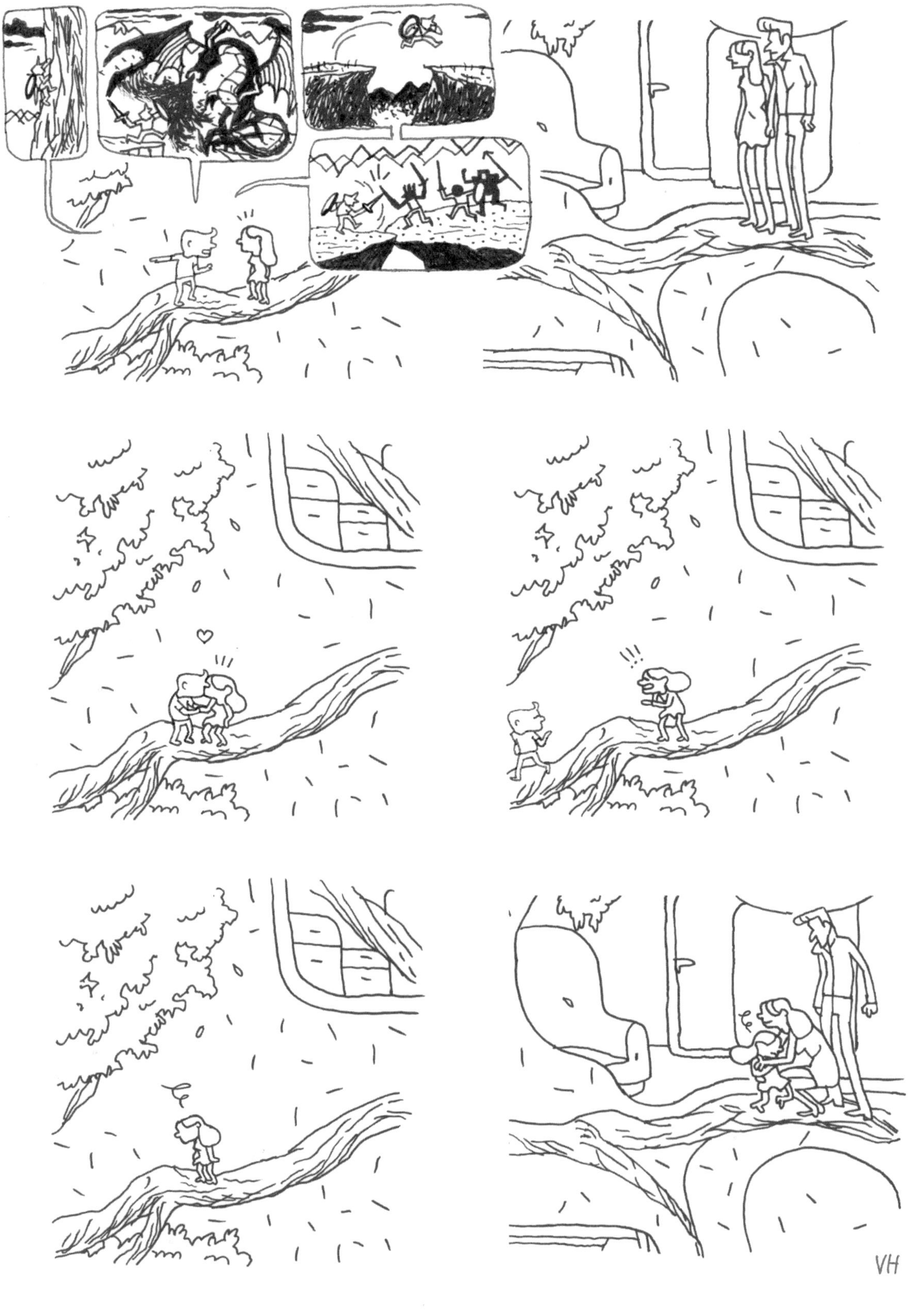

VH

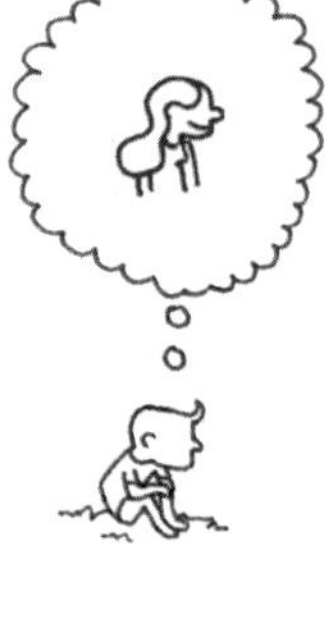

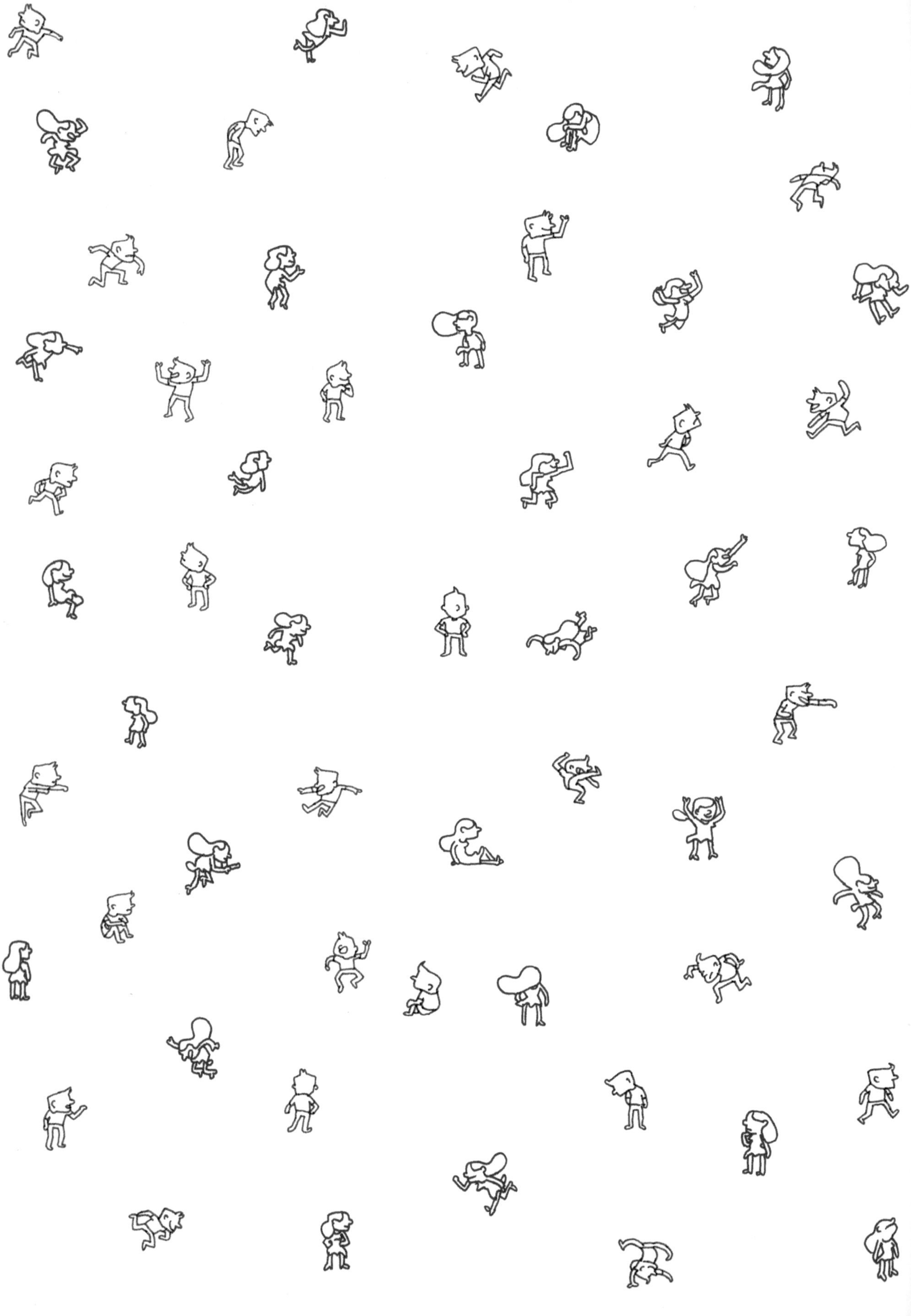